SWEET & SOUR

A MODERN MPREG FAIRYTALE

COLBIE DUNBAR

TRISHA LINDE

Copyright © 2021 Colbie Dunbar and Trisha Linde
All rights reserved. No portion of this book may be reproduced or used in any manner without written permission. All characters appearing in this work are fictitious. Any resemblance to real persons, living or dead, is purely coincidental.

Cover Designed by Fantasia Frog Design

BOOKS IN THE SERIES

Bad Apple
Sweet & Sour
Burning Bridges

ABOUT THE BOOK

Happily Ever Afters are overrated. Cake is far more satisfying.

Omega Bellamy knows better than anyone how food can heal the heart and soothe the soul. Since the death of his omega father, working in their family's diner has been the only thing to bring him any kind of solace. Deep down, though, he knows that there has to be more to life than these worn floors and the handful of regular customers. Unfortunately, with the hospital bills piling up, and deadlines looming, it looks like his future may already be decided.

As a restaurant chain mogul, alpha Larkin is surrounded by everything he could ever possibly want… except his heart's desire. Money and fame mean nothing without someone to share it with, but greed and arrogance are hard habits to break, and he's convinced that no omega will ever be able to see past his flaws.

Larkin is in the process of buying out the local competition when he overhears Bellamy and his alpha father talking about their emotional burden. Struck by a sudden case of guilty conscience, he proposes a solution that could benefit them all. He will help them get back on their feet in exchange for Bellamy working in Larkin's new restaurant. The alpha needs help with new recipes. And because he knows Bellamy would never fall for him, he figures seeing the omega every day is the closest he'll get to a relationship. But he wouldn't say no to more.

Sweet & Sour is the second standalone book in the Once Upon an M/M Romance series by Colbie Dunbar and Trisha Linde. With a mixture of knotty heat and sweet treats, Sweet & Sour combines food and fairytales, along with a cast of intriguing characters, including Bellamy's beloved alpha dad who's still mourning the loss of his husband. And Larkin's loyal staff who see through his hunger for power and understand it for what it really is—tragic loneliness. Beauty and the Beast gets an mpreg twist, giving this classic tale a touch of heat, and obviously, a baby. Because what fairytale is complete without a happily ever after?

CHAPTER 1

BELLAMY

My heart was heavy, grief sneaking up on me as I stood at the diner entrance. It didn't just tap me on the shoulder or wave as it passed by. It tackled me to the ground and pummeled me, and I gave up and let it do its thing.

That was the internal me. Public me plastered a smile on my face and greeted my regular customers. "Good evening, Joe. Adam." Seeing the pair, hand in hand and so much in love, had my eyes welling up. "So nice to see you again. The usual booth?" They nodded as I blinked the tears away and turned to their kids. "Hi, guys. How are you?"

"Bellamy, guess what?" Not waiting for a response, Todd, the youngest, burst out, "I aced my math test."

"Gimme a high-five." Todd struggled with math, as I had in school, but his parents had hired a tutor—a local high school kid—who'd not only coached him but had approached the subject by doing plenty of hands-on learning and real-life tasks.

"And I got picked for the soccer team," Archie, Todd's older brother, told me proudly.

After another high-five, I explained, "I played soccer too

when I was in elementary school." That had me choking up because Dad, my omega father, had watched all my games, no matter the weather. He and Pop, my alpha dad, were my biggest fans, in sport, at school, and in life. They showed me, rather than told me, I could do anything I wanted. "Dream big, Bellamy," they'd said. It was their mantra, and they'd lived by it.

But my family no longer included a 'they' when talking or thinking about my parents. It was always 'he', and 'they' was consigned to the past, while 'we' was Pop and me.

Making a comment to a passing waiter had me brushing the back of my hand over my cheeks and wiping off the wetness. I hoped no one was paying attention to the crack in my voice as I showed the guests to the booth in the corner.

Sven, the waiter who'd been with us the longest, caught my eye and jerked his head toward the front door where a man was waiting to see me. "I'll leave you in Sven's capable hands," I told Archie and family.

"Hey, Sven, guess what?" Todd again. He was so proud of passing that damn test I wanted to give him a medal.

"Andy," I shook hands with the omega hovering at the entrance, who'd owned and run a small hardware store all of his working life until a major chain had arrived in town and put him out of business. I took him into the kitchen where the staff greeted him. I would have offered him a job but his hands were twisted with arthritis.

Andy was in the process of selling his house and moving in with his daughter, but until the sale went through, he was hard up for cash and was too proud to tell his family or ask the bank for a bridging loan.

"Here you go." I handed him two large bags, meals enough for three days, including dessert and soup.

"I'll pay you back, you know," Andy said, his rheumy eyes blinking and fluttering.

"And the best way to do that is enjoy this food and look

after yourself." An offer had been put in on the sale of his home, but the paperwork involved when selling a house often took longer than expected and there had been hiccups in the process.

Making sure Andy had a ride home distracted me from my own pain. But as I pushed away the sadness and headed toward the kitchen, a hand clapped me on the shoulder. "Bellamy!" The familiar voice had me cringing and shrinking away from the alpha whose breath was heaving over my neck. *I don't need this today!*

"W-Winston," I stammered. "Are you eating in?" As soon as the words were out of my mouth I regretted them. *God, I'm so stupid.*

"I'd love to." Warm breath on my ear had my stomach churning. "Is there a back room we can use?"

I flung his meaty hand off me. "You know what I mean." Without glancing around, I added, "We're pretty busy today, why don't you get your food to go." There was no need to show him a menu, he ordered the same thing whenever he came in.

"Ahhh, Bellamy, where's the fun in that?" He stuck out his tongue and licked his lips, and I pictured that tongue on me, sliding over my cheek. *Gross!*

Winston never took no for an answer, despite me repeating the word countless times. He was one of those alphas who assumed his status gave him carte blanche when it came to relationships. Not that we would ever have a relationship other than creepy customer and disgruntled diner owner/operator.

"I'll wear you down, don't worry. One day you'll realize what you've been missing." He grabbed his crotch and cupped the bulge in his pants. *Disgusting.*

"Stay here and I'll get your food."

He pouted which was childish for a grown man. "Don't leave me."

I ignored him, wishing I could get a restraining order. "Can we have a bacon cheeseburger and fries?" I poked my head in the kitchen, eager to get away from Winston. I'd hate to see the inside of the alpha's arteries, because he never ordered anything green.

"You need to tell that creep to take a hike, boss man." Danny was flipping burgers, a white towel tucked into his waistband, not over his shoulder. He claimed any so-called chef who put their towel over their shoulder was half-assing his job and was doing it for show. He told me once if I ever hired a towel-over-the-shoulder guy, he'd walk. He'd throw down his ladle and knife, fling off his apron, and flounce off through the swinging doors.

It was a running joke between us whenever I had to hire new staff, and I'd taunt him, pretending the new employee insisted on the towel on the shoulder thing.

But the voices of customers and wait staff out front faded and were replaced by the shouts and urgent requests of the cooks and kitchen hands. Beef stock bubbled on a gas burner as the bluish flame glowed beneath the huge pot, while bacon sizzled on the other side of the kitchen. In the midst of the frenzied sounds of a typical lunch hour, I noted the familiar cracking of eggs, and the comforting aroma of chili wafted over me from a simmering stainless-steel pot.

This was my comfort zone. No matter how hectic, no matter if I was splattered with tomato sauce or if a plate shattered on the linoleum floor. This was my safe space. I'd grown up here. Did my homework in the back room if we were busy or out front if things were slow. Tasted Dad's experiments, some of which made it onto the menu while others didn't.

Pop worked out front—he wasn't much of a cook—but he was great with the customers. Knew how to schmooze when he had to, sensed when tissues and a shoulder to cry on were needed, and deftly sidestepped potential customer complaints. But he remembered everyone's story. Today was his day off or he would have headed Winston off at the pass. And I would've been in the kitchen.

I put on my favorite apron as Rob, a kitchen hand/waiter/trainee chef, handed me a paper bag, but Danny snatched it out of his hand and stomped into the restaurant.

"But I expected Bellamy to bring me my lunch," a pitiful voice yelled. "Bellamy? Bellamy? I'll be back tomorrow and I might shock you with a different lunch order."

Danny pushed through the swinging doors, a grim expression on his face. "That guy needs to get laid."

"Maybe we should hook him up with someone," Rob suggested. "You know, like a blind date."

"I wouldn't do that to my worst enemy." Danny slammed an empty pot on the stainless counter. "Rob, are you keeping an eye on the brownies?"

"On it." The young chef hurried off.

"Seriously, boss. You need to tell Winston to take a hike."

"The only one he wants to take is with me." And once again, memories of hiking with Dad and Pop had me fighting back tears.

Chocolate pie. I had to make one. That was Dad's favorite, and the three of us would sit at a booth, late at night, each with a spoon, attacking the remains of creamy pie.

Making pastry was one of the first recipes Dad shared with me. My first attempt had been so tough and inedible we'd tossed it. But now I could do this in my sleep. Flour and salt, add butter until the mixture crumbled, and then ice-cold water. I'd made some earlier and got it out of the fridge.

And now for my favorite part. Rolling it out. And as I did, the memories of Dad stretched before me as the dough extended and flattened. My heart wept, remembering my omega dad. His death left a huge hole in our lives and at the diner.

CHAPTER 2

LARKIN

"Morning, Mr. Badeaux, sir."

I gave a nod to the man, since that was easier than actually replying to him. If I answered with words, that implied I was interested in talking, and then there was the potential of being forced to engage in conversation. Heaven forbid! And then I might end up being forced to admit that I could never remember his name.

Or any of their names, for that matter.

Lucky for me, my staff knew better. The greeting had been nothing more than a formality. And as I swept through the kitchen—clean, bright, white and gleaming—I was buffeted with muffled greetings and pleasantries, but their eyes always skittered away. Their lack of interest matched my own. I may be the owner of this establishment, but I was no chef. It was an investment opportunity, nothing more.

I straightened my lapels and basked, for one simple moment, in my domain. Just one of many domains, in fact. I owned a dozen restaurants across the state, though this was my most lucrative. Larkin Badeaux was practically a household name when it came to the food industry. I was at the pinnacle of my career.

Nowhere to go but down, a small voice murmured in my mind.

Hush up, I snapped at myself. I was still young, bold, hard-working. I practically held the world in the palm of my hand. Except… when I looked down at my palm, it told a different story. The skin of my hands was unblemished, far too smooth. When was the last time I'd even made myself a sandwich? Let alone made a meal for someone else.

The thought had my breath quivering. Was that what I wanted? Someone to cook for? My throat grew tight at the mere suggestion. No. There was no room in my life for anyone. Not now, and maybe not ever.

"Joseph," I called, loud enough to be heard no matter where in the kitchen he was. I held my hand up so he would be able to see me through the steam. My kitchen manager hustled over.

"Yes, sir. Morning, sir," he said with a curt nod. I liked the alpha; he was blunt and to the point, bold enough for the staff to sit up and take notice but not so ambitious as to have a problem taking orders from me.

"Sales?" I enquired.

"Down 2% this quarter, but up from last week."

His answer brought an involuntary frown to my lips. Down? Again? "Reservations tonight?"

"13, sir. The mayor's assistant has requested a table for seven o'clock, and…"

His hesitation had me darting my eyes to take in his posture. He bit his lip, and I snapped, "What is it? A problem with the lunch rush?"

"No, sir, quite the opposite. We have a food critic from *Yum!* magazine at table eight."

My heart gave a little patter of excitement, first at the mention of this evening's esteemed guest—the mayor was a big spender, and he always tweeted with pictures of his meal, it would be great advertising—but it was the second piece of news that had my stomach roiling. "Who's the critic?"

"Maria Tristov."

No. Not that bitch. This could be disastrous. "Did you make her meal?" I snarled.

"Yes, sir. Of course." Though the set of his shoulders said he was confident in the food he'd prepared for her, there was something uneasy skittering across his eyes, and it left me feeling cold.

Without another word, I left Joseph standing there and swept out of the kitchen into the main dining room, grabbing a bottle of red wine on the way. Table eight was smack dab in the middle of the spacious dining room. It was bright and sunny at this time of day, but out of the direct glare. It was a good choice of table to seat her. However, as I looked around the room, I was left feeling more than a little uneasy. There were far too many empty tables for the middle of the lunch rush.

"Good afternoon, Miss Tristov," I said softly, bringing the bitch's eyes up. They hardened at the sight of me. "I trust everything is well with your meal?"

Her lips pursed as if she'd tasted something sour. "It is… sufficient."

Sufficient? What was that supposed to mean? I looked down to where her meal had barely been touched. "Can I interest you in a glass of wine?" Wouldn't hurt to liquor the woman up, grease my way into a good review.

"I'll pass, thanks. It's a bit early for drinking."

"Very well then." I was about to turn away, but her cold demeanor and callous attitude were itching at me, I just couldn't help myself. "Excuse me, Miss Tristov, I can't help but ask… is there anything wrong with your meal? You haven't eaten much, and I would be remiss if I didn't ensure the utmost satisfaction of my customers."

She dabbed at her mouth with her napkin and then threw

it down beside her plate. "The food is edible. I would normally eat more than this, but I had breakfast at Bel's Diner this morning and ate way too much. I couldn't seem to stop myself." She gave me a thin smile that somehow indicated that we had nothing else to discuss.

I plastered on a demure smile over my gritted teeth and politely made my way back towards the kitchen, but before I could pass through the doors, I couldn't help but overhear a couple at another table. "Did you hear that? Sounds like Bel's Diner is the place to be. Have you tried it?"

"Oh yeah, that place is amazing! The food is to die for, not to mention way cheaper than this overpriced meal. The staff's awesome too. Family-run, if you can believe it. Super cute."

"Why didn't we go there for lunch?"

The swinging door whooshed closed behind me, cutting off their conversation, but their words kept echoing through my mind. Bel's Diner…

I wish I could say this was the first I'd heard of them, but it wasn't. Not by a long shot. Over the past few years, they seemed to keep coming up in conversation, and it was nothing but good things. The food? Delicious. The prices? Too low, if you asked my opinion. And the staff… people couldn't stop bringing up how friendly the staff was.

Argh! What the hell did they have that my restaurant didn't? We had top-of-the-line kitchen equipment, all the best ingredients money could buy. The recipes we used were all finely honed, award-winning dishes that we'd been making for years. And our staff… My eyes scanned the kitchen and roved over the random faces, all decidedly avoiding my gaze. Well, maybe they weren't the most energetic bunch, I supposed, but what did it matter if the kitchen staff wasn't friendly? It wasn't like the customers could even see them.

Everything was just the way I liked it. Perfect. As always.

Joseph walked up to my side and cleared his throat, waiting until I turned to acknowledge him. "What is it?" I barked.

Joseph looked reluctant to speak.

"Spit it out, already. I have better things to do than hang around here."

"Well, sir… it's just… the mayor's assistant has just called."

"Uh huh."

"They've cancelled their reservation."

Shit.

CHAPTER 3

BELLAMY

Plonking myself in the booth, I sipped from a huge mug of milky sweet tea. It was my go-to drink at the end of a shift when coffee would have kept me up most of the night. To be honest, I preferred my tea with lemon, but Dad had always drunk it this way, and my doing the same was an homage to him. Gulping the warm sweet liquid put a smile on my face.

I leaned my head back on the padded bench, bone tired on the outside, missing Dad on the inside. Not a day went by that he wasn't in my thoughts. If losing him had taught me one thing it was that the grieving process was different for everyone. It wasn't a straight road. It had bends and curves, steep hills and huge fucking potholes.

I was getting there, and so was Pop. The place we were aiming for wasn't as far away as it had been. We could sort of see it, but we had a ways to go. We wanted to be where we could remember Dad without so much pain.

Pop sat down opposite me, holding a steaming mug and a wad of paper. I assumed they were bills. I put a hand over my face, wishing I could magic them away, but when I peeked between my fingers, they were still there.

"Whatcha got, Pop?" Such a stupid question. It was a lame attempt to postpone the inevitable.

"Hot chocolate." He refused to change his late-night drink of choice no matter the season or the weather. He and Dad had a routine after they closed the diner. Tea and hot chocolate and chatting about their day. Now it was me and Pop. We'd never discussed it but had gravitated toward sitting together, mostly sitting in silence with our memories.

I tapped my fingers against the laminate tabletop as Pop waved the wad of paper at me. "Bills. Not just diner bills or personal ones for the house." I knew what was coming and was tempted to put both hands over my ears. "Hospital and funeral bills."

Oh God! I raked my nails over my scalp, frustrated and angry that having a loved one be in the hospital and die of cancer wasn't bad enough. They had to bleed us dry with exorbitant charges for his care.

Money for the funeral was different. It was a day where Dad's loved ones celebrated his life. Though a niggling thought had me wondering if the funeral company took advantage of bereaved families and gouged them. *Stop with the negative thoughts, Bellamy. Dad would hate that and it's not helping Pop.* Or me.

Pop reached out and covered my hand with his. "Nor sure we can keep going like this. The diner isn't doing well enough to cover what we owe. We're sinking under a mountain of debt, love." His eyes glistened with unshed tears and his hands lined with light blue veins trembled.

No. I didn't want to hear talk like that. "I can get a second job. Work late nights and early mornings as a... a..." I stumbled over the words as I mentally went over a list of my skills. Being a chef and running the diner were pretty much all I knew how to do. "I could clean offices or work as a security guard. Or data entry. That could be done from home.

Maybe get a gig on a local newspaper writing a weekly column."

That last one was a half-assed suggestion. No one wanted cooking advice from a guy who flipped burgers and made teddy bear pancakes for kids who'd passed a math test.

"Son, I appreciate what you're trying to do, but you can't work all day and evening and then go straight to a second job. You'd get maybe three hours of sleep if you're lucky. You'd end up slacking in both jobs, not doing either well."

"Then we have to turn the diner business around. Come up with ways to bring in more customers. Maybe cater to parties—kids' parties—and conduct cooking classes on Sundays. Bring in a new menu. Make more healthy food. Add some vegetarian dishes." I rubbed a hand over my face, admitting in my heart that the suggestions weren't enough.

"We have vegetarian dishes. And vegan. Salad. Fries. Ummm mushroom soup." His mouth turned up. Now he was just fucking with me. "Sweetheart, the answer won't be found in us killing ourselves…" He paused and gulped. "Sorry, wrong choice of words." He shoved the bills with his elbow and they slid over the tabletop, some floating onto the floor. "Maybe we have to…"

I interrupted him, not wanting to hear the words. Once they'd been said, they couldn't be unsaid. "Please don't, Pop. Dad would have done everything possible to keep his dream alive."

"True. But he's not here. And he would never forgive us for trying to prop up the business when we have no hope of saving it."

I pummeled my fists on the table. "No, Pop. There has to be another way. I refuse to sell the diner. We can't let it go. I won't."

He sighed and glanced around at the room. The walls were covered with framed photos. Many were of our regular and much-loved customers. But the pics were mostly of me.

Dad pregnant with me. Me as a newborn in Pop's arms. My first birthday with Pop and Dad blowing out the candles and me fisting a huge chunk of cake and shoving it in my mouth. Holidays and my high school graduation. So many memories.

"I won't give up without a fight, Pop."

"I get that, but it takes a wise man to know when to quit."

"No one is quitting just yet." I had no idea how we'd pay the hospital. I hoped they had a payment plan. One that continued for the rest of my life 'cause that was how long it'd take to pay off the mounting debt.

The front door jingled. *Damn! Did I forget to lock it?* "We're closed," Pop and I yelled.

"Sorry. I didn't mean to interrupt." A voice that reminded me of shimmering strands of syrup being twirled around a spoon and spiraling through the air onto a pancake vibrated through the room.

It occurred to me it might have been a homeless guy looking for food or even somewhere to sleep, but the confidence behind that voice told me he had a place to lay his head and his stomach wasn't rumbling from hunger.

I half rose from the table and noted Pop frowning. Did he think the guy was coming to steal the day's takings? "Can I help you?" I'd turned off most of the lights except the one over the booth where Pop and I were sitting. I could only see the guy's shadow, outlined against the streetlight from outside.

"We might be able to help one another." He paused.

"Sorry, we're not hiring." We could barely pay the staff we had and no one had gotten a raise in a while.

"You misunderstand me." He took a step closer. Tall, dark-haired. His face was in shadow. Was he handsome as well? "I couldn't help overhearing what you were discussing."

CHAPTER 4

LARKIN

*O*verhearing was too kind a word for what I had been doing. Eavesdropping might've been more accurate. Or snooping…

I had come down to Bel's Diner this evening with little more than a ghost of a plan. It was pure curiosity, at this point. I didn't dare to admit that I felt threatened by this tiny, cheap diner, with its poorly chosen location and its kitschy character. I'd just wanted to come in for a meal, snap a few pictures of the décor, and maybe walk out with a copy of the menu. But when I'd arrived, I was greeted with a packed diner, each table filled with smiling faces, and a line of people waiting, right out the door. And the aroma! The air itself danced against my tongue; I could practically taste the food before I'd even put a bite in my mouth.

One glance at the young, sexy omega stepping out of the kitchen had me turning on my heel and walking straight back out the door. I wasn't prepared for any of this. My senses were on total overload, what with the sounds, smells, and downright erotic feelings stirring in me all at once. Stepping into that diner was akin to foreplay.

And so, I had stood outside, waiting for them to close.

Why? I couldn't have told you. At least, I couldn't describe my actions without sounding like a criminal. I didn't want to break into the place, no. I wasn't about to stoop to burglary, but standing next to an open window and listening to the owners talk? Nothing illegal about that. Right?

When they'd started to talk about their mound of debt, it made me feel... despicable, because the first thing that hit me was satisfaction. It was like a dream come true! All I would have to do was wait, and time would do all the hard work for me. The diner would close and I would once again have the corner market.

I gritted my teeth against the squirming guilt I felt in my gut. I didn't want to be the type of guy who would profit from someone else's misfortune... but... what could I do about it? It was inevitable.

Before I could stop myself, and certainly without any real amount of thought, I walked straight in through the door.

"We might be able to help one another." The words pushed themselves past my lips. Help? I didn't help people, that wasn't who I was. I had clawed my way to the top without any help from anyone. If you couldn't do something yourself, then where was the challenge? Where was the satisfaction in knowing you had achieved it all on your own?

But as I stepped forward, the omega I'd seen earlier stood up from his spot at the booth. I swore my knees wobbled. Now that the grill in the kitchen was cold, there were no competing scents to disguise the man's aroma. And it was even more mouth-watering than the food had been. Like cinnamon and apple pie. And with his brown curly hair hanging down about his face, and those all too adorable freckles scattered about his cheekbones, he wasn't hard to look at either.

"Sorry, we're not hiring."

I shuddered at the thought of working here, no doubt wearing a stained apron. "You misunderstand me," I said, stepping forward and out of the shadows. I could feel the omega's eyes assessing me, and subconsciously puffed up my chest for his approval. Gods, such a damn alphahole stance. What was I doing, preening for him? "I couldn't help overhearing what you were discussing. And I have a solution for you that will benefit us both."

He narrowed his eyes at me. It was obvious he didn't trust me as far as he could throw me, but could I blame him? I was a stranger walking into their diner after hours, uninvited, and I could feel his gaze roaming the tattoos that graced my skin.

"No, thanks," he said shortly, but the older man stood up from the table, interrupting him.

"Now, just hold on, Bellamy. Is that how we treat a guest?"

"A guest!" Bellamy scoffed.

"What else would he be? Besides, if he has a potential solution to our little problem, then don't you think we owe it to your dad to hear him out?" Bellamy's lips pinched, but he said nothing further. The older man turned to me and gave a beckoning gesture with his hand. "Come, why don't you join us. Coffee?"

"Please," I said simply. Everyone knew diner coffee was the best you could find. And sure enough, as I scooted into the booth, a warm aromatic mug of coffee was placed in front of me. I breathed in and confirmed that it was, indeed, better than the coffee I served at my restaurant.

The older alpha urged his son to sit back and down, and then settled in beside him, the two of them eyeing me from across the table, one with suspicion and the other with bold curiosity. The father reached out and offered a hand. "Saul Morley."

"Larkin Badeaux," I replied, shaking his hand.

"French?"

"In name, perhaps, but don't ask me to speak the language."

"Fair enough," he chuckled. "So, why don't you tell us why you were eavesdropping and what you're here to offer."

He didn't appear angry with me. In fact, his gaze was shrewd and calculating. I found I liked this alpha's matter-of-fact attitude very much. I gave him a slow nod. "You need money. I have money."

Bellamy blew out a breath. "Yeah, as if it's as simple as that. What's the catch?"

His father placed a hand on Bellamy's arm and then said to me, "Is it a loan you're offering? I have no interest in going even further into debt."

"How about a business partner?" I offered, but Bellamy was already shaking his head.

"This restaurant is my omega dad's dream. He worked his butt off to get this place off the ground, spent countless hours working in that kitchen. And he didn't spend his whole life working only to have some stranger walk in and stake a claim on it." His dark eyes were blazing, and if his father weren't blocking him in the booth, I imagine he would have stormed out, not even sparing me a backwards glance.

I caught a tiny glimpse of the grief he was feeling, and it did something to my insides, squirming and urging me to draw the omega into my arms, to ease his sadness. I all but shoved that feeling straight back where it belonged, locked in the deep recesses of my mind. There was nothing between us, nor would there ever be.

I held both my hands up, placating. "Okay, I understand. How about…" I couldn't believe I was about to make this offer. It seemed ludicrous! There was no way they would agree. "How about you come to work for me at my restaurant, and I'll pay off the debt."

Now both of the men across from me were chuckling darkly. "Seriously," Saul said, shaking his head. "I'm sorry, but I don't think you fully understand our situation. You could hire any kitchen staff you want off the street. Hell, you could probably hire yourself a 3-star chef with 20 years' experience, and they still wouldn't cost nearly as much as what we owe."

No, it was more like they didn't understand *my* situation. I had money to burn, and I could spend it however I pleased. No, my dilemma wasn't a lack of money… it was my pride. I couldn't stand to have critics sneer at my food. I hated to overhear my customers comparing my restaurant to a two-bit diner. Even if it cost me a small fortune, winning back my reputation was more than worth it to me.

I placed both hands flat on their cheap tabletop, chipped and stained from years of use. I needed to make this offer impossible for them to turn down. I needed to make it seem a fair trade. "Look… I'm trying to make some changes in my restaurant, bring in some new recipes, a whole new vibe. How about I pay the debt, and in exchange, I get a copy of all your recipes… and Bellamy will come with me for one month. He will work in my restaurant and live in my home. He will show me how to prepare the food, walk me through the ingredients you purchase, and give me any pointers."

"Why the hell would I live with you?" Bellamy snapped. "You're so full of yourself."

I narrowed my gaze at him. "The distance is too great for an easy commute. Besides, if I'm going to invest this kind of cash, you can be sure I'm going to get my money's worth." Bellamy's eyes widened, and he was about to lay into me about the sexual innuendo in my suggestion. "Oh please, now who's full of himself," I cut him off. "I meant only that you could give me some private cooking lessons in your off time."

This felt wrong on so many levels. I turned to Saul, and even though I was directing this offer to him, it was truly a decision for Bellamy to make, not his father. I could see his jaw drop from the corner of my eye.

Saul was shaking his head, a dark cloud moving over his expression. "My son is not for sale."

"I didn't mean—" I began to reiterate that I had no untoward expectations, but he was already standing.

"I think you should leave," he said, barely restrained rage clear in his voice.

"You're out of options! Why would you give up on your diner so easily, when I'm giving you a way out?"

"Call it pride or call it self-respect, but I refuse to bend to your ridiculous demands," he seethed, tapping his finger into my chest.

I bit back my reply. It was obvious that I had turned him against me. There was nothing I could say that would change his mind. I had insulted them, shitting on any chance I'd had of an agreement with them. I gave a nod and headed for the door.

I muttered darkly, "I guess I'll just snatch up the property when I hear you've gone belly up. Looks like it's win-win for me. And only lose for you."

I was halfway through the doorway when Bellamy called out, "I'll do it."

"But, son—" his father began, but Bellamy cut him off.

"It's a deal. I'll come with you."

My heart soared and my stomach plummeted. I had no doubt I was going to regret this.

CHAPTER 5

BELLAMY

"You don't have to do this, Bel."

I placed my hands on Pop's shoulders. "It's one month. 31 days and our debts will be paid."

"But that man… he might… it could be… nothing is worth that, and Dad would have agreed with me." Poor man. He couldn't say what he feared Larkin expected from me. He shook me off and clasped one of my hands between both of his. "Giving him all our recipes, all those secrets, in return for getting out of debt is not worth it."

"We'll make new recipes, Pop. And new memories along with the old ones."

But he ignored me and continued. "Plus you… you being in his house. No matter what he says, I suspect he thinks you'll be so grateful, you'll fall at his feet."

"Not naked, I hope," I blurted out and instantly regretted it.

Pop screwed up his face. "Ewww! Don't say that, now I can't get an image of him…"

"Shhh! You forget I'm a grown man and can look after myself." What I didn't say was how much Larkin had affected me when he waltzed into the diner. So many mixed emotions. Shock. Fury. Disbelief, and though I didn't want to admit it, even to myself, relief. But there was something else hiding among the others. Just a hint. A glimpse. A peek.

The alpha's presence had heat pulsing through my veins. The impact was similar to a steamy kitchen with huge pots of stock and soup bubbling on the stove. A heat so powerful it had almost taken away my ability to speak and to reason. And I didn't welcome it. The opposite. I responded with anger.

No one guessed. Not Pop and not him. I was certain they hadn't picked up on my arousal. Sweat trickled down my spine and his aroma threatened to overpower me. I pictured it slithering into my chest and wrapping itself around my heart like a tropical vine.

Shaking my head to rid myself of that memory, I picked up my bag and hugged Pop. "I'll talk to you tonight." He nibbled a fingernail as he saw me out and kept waving from the door until I drove around a corner in my poor beat-up old car and out of sight.

And that was when I pulled over and rested my head on the steering wheel. The calmness and confidence I'd shown in front of my father crumbled. *What the ever loving fuck am I doing?*

Opening the door, I swung my legs onto the ground and put my head between my knees. Breathe in. Breathe out. I was doing this for my late dad. For our loyal staff. For Pop. Having our debt wiped clean, it was practically a fairytale dream come true. I could get through it.

Pulling up out front of the restaurant, I sat with the engine running, taking in the exterior, so unlike the diner with its lopsided neon sign I'd been meaning to fix for ages but never got around to it. This restaurant offered valet parking, but as it was early and the place wasn't open, there were no valet attendants in sight.

As I pushed open the double-sided front door, my eyes

darted around, noting the bland colors on the walls, the tablecloths, table decorations, napkins. Everything was either beige, a light gray, or pristine white. The floor was spotless. No cracks or stains. I could probably eat off it.

A huge contrast with the diner with its black-and-white checkered floor and red upholstered bench and stools. Our place might not be fancy, but it was alive. With tastes, aromas, and the constant sound of laughter. It had life. This place, La Belle Compagne, reminded me of a meal that had gone cold and quickly been warmed up, hoping no one would notice.

"Bellamy!" he took me by surprise. The voice. The one that reminded me of syrup. I steeled myself not to react and turned, hand outstretched, a smile on my face. "You came."

"That was the agreement, wasn't it?" We'd signed the papers yesterday and Larkin had deposited half the money in our account. The rest would be handed over at the end of the month. 31 days of torture. No, I was exaggerating. But I'd be working both in the restaurant and in Larkin's home. Not as some sort of boy toy as Pop had assumed. No matter how much I wanted to save Bel's Diner, prostituting myself was not on the list.

Larkin wanted us to test recipes beforehand, so by the time we put them on the menu, we'd have perfected the dishes. But what he didn't understand was no matter how detailed a recipe was, how well a chef followed the steps, it would change depending on who was doing the cooking. The indescribable essence, the way a chef stirred, grated, and sifted, that couldn't be copied.

"Of course." His confidence which had faltered a moment ago, returned, and he shook my hand, holding on a tad longer than was necessary. Was that a slight squeeze of the fingers? Or did I imagine it?. "Let me show you around."

The droning of his voice pointed out the crisp linen tablecloths, the flower arrangements, and the maître d's station, and I allowed my mind to drift to Larkin, the man behind the public persona. Of course, I'd checked him out online, I'd done little else since he'd interrupted us that night. Wealthy, influential, and admired. He'd clawed his way through the ranks of restaurant kitchens to get to where he was. And he was single, something that hadn't escaped my notice.

He was taller than his shadow had first suggested when he'd barged into the diner. Dark-haired. A colorful and detailed tattoo sleeve slithering up one arm. And while I'd idly wondered in those few seconds before he showed whether he was handsome, the light revealed sculpted cheekbones, a stubble-covered jaw, and a saunter that reminded me of a cat. A large cat.

"What do you think?"

Oh God, I wanted to blab that his body spoke to me. No, sung to me. And not just a run-of-the-mill pop song. It was an operatic aria. But I batted them away, refusing to admit I was attracted to him physically while loathing everything he stood for. I'd had no choice but to accept his offer—which he knew. Being forced to work with him, or for him, was one thing, but I refused to allow my cock to complicate the so-called relationship.

Without glancing at him, I observed, "You've obviously spent a lot and bought the best of everything." I hoped he picked up on my snarkiness. It wasn't like me to put people down, but I took a detour around my principles when it came to Larkin. He'd thrown money at his restaurant, but it wasn't a complete picture. Just a series of things placed around at random like a bunch of strangers not talking to one another.

But it wasn't the furniture or decorations that would make or break the restaurant. It was the food and the staff. "And here's the kitchen." He pushed open the large swinging doors, his face beaming with pride along with a hesitancy. He was showing me, a diner owner-operator—in whose kitchen we made do when things broke down—this gleaming space where every utensil, machine, and gadget was up-to-the-minute modern. I could shave or do my hair in the reflection of the stainless steel appliances.

But this was a paint-by-numbers restaurant, indistinguishable from countless other places. *Why would anyone choose to come here?* It had no heart, at least not a beating one. It was on life support, and I suspected the only thing that gave it any spark were the staff. They were lined up, a streak of white, slicing through the metallic gray of the kitchen.

"This is Joseph, my kitchen manager."

"Welcome, Mr. Morley." He was polite, overly so, but his posture told another story. A wariness, which was understandable. What had Larkin told them about me? Was I going to usurp them? Give orders? Or worse, fire them.

"Please, call me Bellamy."

Names and positions blurred. "Sous chef, Charlie. Pastry chef, Brian. Prep cook, Polly. Executive chef, Michael." Larkin moved down the line and tugged at one person's collar and told another he had to change his apron as it was stained. Perfectly reasonable for an upmarket kitchen but his gruff manner was off-putting.

I lost count of how many hands I shook as my mind calculated how much it cost to support this many people. And those were just the kitchen staff. The front-of-house staff had not yet arrived.

A man poked his head through the door. "There's a phone call for you, sir."

Larkin huffed and furrowed his brow, clearly not wanting to leave me alone with his employees. "Go," I said. "I'll putter around until you get back."

I was the new kid in school, standing awkwardly, not knowing where to go. But I had to set the staff at ease. It wasn't their fault their boss was an ass. I was furious on their behalf. If that was how Larkin treated his staff, we were going to butt heads every day. "I'm not sure what Larkin has told you, but I'm not here to take anyone's jobs or tell you what to do. I'm not your boss, but your partner."

The relief in the room was palpable.

"We're just hoping to try a few things, but I'll need your help. I'm the new guy fumbling my way around. And please, call me Bellamy. "

"Would you like to see today's delivery, B-Bellamy? Joseph asked.

"I'd love to." As we inspected the beef, chicken, veal, and pork, plus the seasonal vegetables, the staff gathered around and observed me examining each cut of meat and bushel, bunch, and head of vegetables and herbs. "Any suggestions on how we can combine some of these to make new dishes?"

My question was greeted with silence. "Anyone? There are no wrong answers. We're just brainstorming."

"Instead of wiener schnitzel perhaps we could combine the veal and these mushrooms along with herbs and make a veal loaf," Brian suggested.

"Great idea. I like it. Let's make a list and we can pick one or two dishes to experiment with."

After ten minutes, we had a long list, and the tense atmosphere in the kitchen had evaporated. Joseph headed out back to deal with another delivery, and Polly leaned toward me and said, "We were worried when the boss announced you were coming."

Charlie piped up, "We thought you might have bought the place and were kicking him out."

That was never going to happen.

Michael spoke up. "He's not that bad, you know. He might be a grumpy so-and-so, but he's *our* grouchy boss." Heads nodded in agreement.

By the time Larkin returned, we were sharing restaurant horror stories and laughing as each one was more outrageous than the last. All eyes flicked in his direction and everyone scattered back to their stations. He froze, his face registering hurt as though he was the kid left out when everyone else in the class had been invited to a birthday party. *Shit!* The last thing we needed was more tension between us.

CHAPTER 6

LARKIN

It's just like any other day.

At least, that was what I tried to tell myself. Except, on a normal day, I wouldn't be here in the kitchen. This was no longer my job, now that I owned the place. No, instead, I would either be in the back office signing paperwork, traveling the country to investigate (or acquire) other restaurants, or doing some interview for a foodie magazine. Those were secretly my favorite. I was even the city's most eligible bachelor last year, and while I joked about the gazes it brought my way, I had noticed that the media attention was tapering off too quickly.

I hated to admit it, but even though this kitchen technically belonged to me, I didn't feel even slightly comfortable within its walls. It was like an ill-fitting set of pants, too tight around the waist and three inches too short. And just as those pants would leave my ankles cold, I was certainly feeling a little chilly from the looks I was getting from the staff.

"What!" I finally barked at the dishwasher as I caught him sneaking a glance at me over his shoulder.

"What?" he squeaked, spinning around. "Nothing, sir." He

snapped to attention, but he wasn't quite looking me in the eye. More like just a tad too high. My forehead, maybe.

I narrowed my gaze at him, and I wouldn't have been surprised if his knees started knocking together. "Don't you have some dishes to wash?" I sneered.

"Y-yes, sir." He stood a moment longer, then shook himself free of my stare and darted off, collecting knives and utensils that had been set aside on the counter.

Fake it till you make it. That had been the advice of my first boss. My first day as a busser, and I didn't have a single clue what I was doing. The place had been jumping, every table filled and a line at the door. I froze, panicked, and Ross, a barrel-chested beast of a man, had placed a hand gently on my shoulder and had given me that advice. Even though I hadn't been trained, he threw me out into the fray. *Keep your chin up and try to look like you know what you're doing. Nobody out there will know any different.*

20 years later, and I felt like nothing much had changed. His advice could still apply. I held my head high and straightened out my shoulders, and I marched through the kitchen as if I belonged here. As if this wasn't more their domain than mine.

I leaned over the soup pot on the stove and took a deep breath of the steam. Ahhh, delicious. Mellow and yet tangy, a soft orange color. I honestly had no clue what it was.

"Sir, would you… would you like a taste?" A woman appeared at my elbow, a spoon held tentatively out for me. Her curly hair was just barely tamed by the cap on her head. I recognized her, but her name escaped me.

"Yes, I would." One of the first rules of the kitchen was to taste everything. If you were going to serve it to customers, you had to have confidence that it was up to strict standards. I took the spoon and dipped it into the pot. The soup was like nothing I had ever tasted before, but it was everything I'd dreamed it would be. Creamy, salty, spicy. I tried to analyze the flavors, identify the ingredients.

The woman must have seen something on my face, because she offered, "It's tom kha gai, sir. There's chicken, coconut milk—"

"I know what it is," I growled and instantly regretted it. Her expression, which had been carefully opening for me, now shuttered and closed up tight, her eyes darting down to her feet. "We're a French restaurant, and this soup couldn't be further from that. Are we trying to confuse our customers?"

"Sorry, sir," she whispered. "It was Bel—I mean, Mr. Morley's idea."

Of course it was.

I took a small breath and placed my spoon on the counter. "Thank you… Penelope," I made a stab at her name. I was trying, that was what counted… right?

I continued down the line, and just barely heard from behind me, "It's Polly, sir."

I made a note to remember her name, though honestly, I knew it was pointless. The staff despised me, and remembering their names wouldn't change that. But it wasn't my job to be their friend. I couldn't be seen to be on the same level as my staff, it was better if they were terrified of me. It demanded loyalty.

The kitchen staff parted around me like the red sea. All except Bellamy. As everyone cleared away, it left a clear path straight to where the omega was talking with Joseph. I had done my best to keep my distance from Bellamy, with his spiced aroma and his unabashed smile, but seeing how those pants hugged his tight ass, I couldn't seem to stop myself from moving in for a closer look.

Joseph glanced up from where he was leaning on the counter, and seeing me, he quickly stood to attention. "Sir!"

"So… hard at work, are we? Holding up the counter?" I'd

meant for it to be teasing, but by the look on Joseph's face, I knew it had come across more like a wolf offering a toothy grin to a little fluffy bunny.

Joseph gulped, his Adam's apple bobbing. "We were just tweaking the menu, sir."

I frowned down at the piece of paper on the counter between them. "Yes. I see that." I wedged myself in, turning to face Bellamy, until Joseph got the hint and made himself scarce. "Do you want to tell me why none of these dishes are French? I run a French restaurant, after all."

I could have fallen into Bellamy's eyes, their rich chocolate depths, but then I realized that he was the first person in this kitchen to look me directly in the eye, and I sobered quickly from my daze. And his look wasn't warm and welcoming, but bold, daring me to say something. He was no doubt up for the challenge.

"You hired me to make changes. Well, French wasn't working for you. So, I figured we would try a few different menus and see which one got the best reception."

"You should have cleared it with me first."

His lips twitched, and I wasn't sure if it was with a smile… or a sneer. "Of course. You're right." We stood in our standoff, breathing deeply, for just a beat too long, before he said, "So… is that okay with you, *sir*?"

The way he called me sir was most definitely mocking, but I couldn't help the way it stirred something deep inside me. A heat, deep in my gut. I could get used to him calling me sir. And then, suddenly, that ill-fitting-pants feeling was back, except now it was because of the semi I was sporting.

"Yes," I said, clearing my throat and trying to keep his attention on my face so he wouldn't look down and get the wrong impression. I didn't hire him for any reason except for his skills in a kitchen. That was the *only* reason. "I look forward to seeing what you come up with."

I began to walk away, planning to retreat to my office to

maybe get this arousal taken care of, but Bellamy stopped me. "Actually, Larkin, can you help me for a quick sec? I can't seem to find your bacon stretcher."

"Our bacon... stretcher?"

"Yeah, if I'd known you didn't have one, I would have brought my own."

There wasn't a single kitchen appliance or utensil we didn't have. I'd spared no expense for my business. There was no way that the tiny diner of his had something we did not. "I'm sure it's here somewhere. I'll track it down for you."

The smile he offered me was more than worth the effort. "Thanks, Larkin. You're a huge help."

I spent half an hour looking through the shelves before I finally broke down and asked Joseph where the bacon stretcher was.

"Sir, there's... no such thing as a bacon stretcher," he said, his eyes skittering away.

Oh. I felt like such a fool.

I looked back through the kitchen at Bellamy, only to find him leaning back against the counter watching me, his arms folded across his chest. He gave me a wink and bit his lip to hold back his outright grin.

So that's how this is going to be. I marched into the office without a backward glance, and the moment I slammed the door, I heard the kitchen staff erupt into laughter. At my expense. It had been one day, and already Bellamy had turned my loyal staff against me. One day down, only 30 to go.

His food had damn well better be fucking amazing.

They let me stew in my office for a good hour. I paced, I growled, but no matter what I did, it couldn't erase the way he'd made me feel. How had I ever found that ogre attractive? Ugh.

Then a soft knock came at the door. "What!" I shouted.

It cracked open and Joseph peeked one eye through the crack. "Sir?"

"What do you want, Joseph?" I snapped, rounding the desk to throw myself into my chair.

He stepped tentatively into the room and eased the door shut behind him. "Excuse the interruption, Mr. Badeaux, sir, I just wanted to tell you a story about—"

"It isn't storytime, Joseph. Don't you have work to do?"

He held his hand up and gave me a look that said to be patient for a minute. "I wanted to tell you about the time I was sent to find the bacon stretcher."

"You—" Had he come in here to mock me? To rub my nose in my blunder?

"Sir, I know this is hard to believe, but this is a rite of passage. It's a kind of… initiation into the kitchen. We've all been there. The staff… they're not laughing at you, sir. They're laughing at the memory of their own experiences. It's a good-natured ribbing. Mr. Morley has done you a favor."

I blew a breath out through my lips. "Oh really? And what favor would that be?"

"He made you more human, sir." Joseph gave me a soft smile and then backed his way out the door, leaving me to my thoughts.

More human? Hadn't I been human enough?

CHAPTER 7

BELLAMY

"Would someone tell me what in the fuck bi bop bum is?" Larkin was standing in the doorway with what I assumed was today's menu in his hand. There were sniggers, and Larkin frowned as a number of the staff took one look at his face and dropped something. They then fell to the floor and stayed there, stifling giggles with their hand. Someone else stuck their head in one of the kitchen's huge industrial fridges, while a couple of others raced to the storeroom.

"I mean bap bum bibi." He tossed the menu aside. "Shit! How do I pronounce this and what in the hell is it? Before you arrived, Bellamy, people knew how to read the dishes on the menu."

"Because everyone speaks perfect French," I mumbled under my breath. With a smile on my face, I explained, "It's a well-known Korean dish. Very popular. Quite simple but a great combination of flavors," and I placed the recipe in front of him.

"I will not have a dish on the menu named after someone's ass." He screwed up his face as though someone had just farted.

"Agreed. 100%. That would be bad," I said as I chewed my bottom lip, desperate not to laugh. "It's bibimbap. No bottoms or butts in sight." Well, maybe one. Larkin was leaning over the counter, ass in the air as he stabbed at the recipe. It took all my strength not to put my hand on his butt. The kitchen was full of possibilities and deliciousness but none were as delectable as that alpha's behind.

Bellamy! I hated myself for the feelings bubbling out of me. How could I be attracted to that vile man? And what did that say about me? I was a horrible person. That was the only answer.

Damn! I'd tried to live my life being kind to others, working hard, and being what I thought was a good person. So, how did everything flip and put me on the wrong side of the fence? That was a question for another time. Right now I had some explaining to do.

"It's made with beef. I use ground beef, and plenty of vegetables, rice, and a yummy sauce. Here." I grabbed a small bowl and spoon. "This is the sauce. Have a taste and guess what's in it."

A wary expression came over him and he glanced around at the faces of the staff who'd gotten over the giggles and now had their eyes glued on their boss.

"Don't worry," I assured him. "It tastes nothing like…"

"Ass," everyone shouted.

"If you're trying to make me feel better, it's not working." He put his hands on his hips and glared at everyone.

"Try it," I urged him.

Holding my breath, hoping he wouldn't throw an adult-sized tantrum, I fixed my gaze on the spoon as he lifted it to his mouth." Perfect and plump. And pink. His lips, not the spoon. He sipped a tiny amount and a range of emotions flashed over his face. Was that confusion or discomfort?

"G-Garlic," he stammered.

"Yes. Anything else?"

He fanned his face. "Something spicy. Chili. But different."

"Mmmm. It's a chili paste," I explained. "A Korean one."

He took another sip and licked around his mouth. A vision popped into my head of his tongue in my mouth, poking it in my ear and licking pre-cum off my dick. I white-knuckled the bowl as sweat dotted my upper lip.

"There's a definite hint of sesame." His grin let me know he'd gotten more confident, and I wasn't going to shame him for not picking out the different flavors. "I like it. Different. Bursting with flavor."

"Glad you like it. Charlie will be making that today."

Slowly, slowly new items had crept onto the menu. We'd try new dishes, not too many. We didn't want to overwhelm the customers. Some were bound to be more successful than others. Some would become permanent while others would be shuffled around. A few would no doubt disappear without a trace.

"Well, I'll leave you to it. Seems as though you have everything under control."

He swept out of the kitchen with me at his heels. "Larkin." But he had his phone tucked under his ear, and I tugged at his sleeve. He swirled around and I took a step back. "You should join us."

One brow shot up. "For what?"

"To cook."

"The ass dish?"

Oh God. If he said that in front of a customer, he may as well close the restaurant. The most successful businessmen didn't put their foot in their mouth. "No. I was planning on making vegetarian tagine."

That was another direction I was pursuing. Adding a couple of vegetarian dishes to cater to a wider clientele. And I was thinking of making sure there were dishes for people with food allergies. Slowly, slowly.

"Come and help me. It'll be good to get your hands dirty." I so wanted him dirty, covered in sweat and my slick. And naked. My face burned and I glanced at a clock on the wall hoping he wasn't paying attention to the flush on my cheeks.

"I have paperwork to deal with."

"How long has it been since you worked in a kitchen? That's where a dish comes to life. How can you expect to reflect your passion and enthusiasm for the food to the customers if you haven't been part of the process from the beginning?"

His eyes darted around the dining room, looking anywhere but at me. "Fine."

He followed me into the kitchen, and I told him, "This is my own mixture made up of twelve different spices."

"You're not going to make me identify each one, are you?"

"Nah, you're good. Also, this is a much quicker version of a tagine. Done on the stove."

He rolled up his sleeves, revealing his tattoos, and I handed him an apron. "So, what is this tagine we're making?"

"Pumpkin and couscous. You're on chopping duty to start with."

He hesitated before choosing a knife, and when he glanced around the kitchen, everyone got very busy. Without standing over him, I kept an eye on his chopping technique from a distance as he cut the onions, ginger, and garlic. It was obvious he knew what he was doing, but he'd been sitting behind a desk and glad-handing wealthy customers and restaurant critics for too long.

But I winced as he came close to cutting his finger. The usual babble of voices was cut off as everyone held their breath. I waved my arms and made a don't-look-at-him face. Polly put a finger to her lips and pointed at the first-aid kit.

Larkin eventually finished his chopping and then cooked the ingredients until they were soft. Once he was done, I tossed in my spice mixture. And suddenly, the kitchen was transformed from a modern facility that churned out food to a far-flung desert with the sun sinking over the horizon. I imagined the fierce daytime heat being replaced by the cool temperatures of the barren landscape and me warming my hands by the fire.

"Wow! That's some combination of flavors." Larkin flapped his hand over the pot and sniffed. Now he was there with me in that desert. *I wish.* "That's amazing."

"Glad you like it."

Larkin busied himself with stirring while I added ingredients, each of us tasting as we went. Some of the sauce dribbled over his chin and he wiped it off with a towel. "Did I get it all off?"

Wrong question, Larkin. Time for me to have fun. I tapped the end of my nose. "You have a spot right here."

He wiped the tip of his nose. "Now?"

"Still there."

From the corner of my eye, I noted Micheal studying us as Larkin rubbed a hand over his nose. He stared at his palm. "Nothing."

"Oops. Must have been mistaken."

He squinted at me and pursed his lips. "Were you jerking me around, Bellamy?" *Yes, but I'd love to jerk you in other ways too.* A glimmer of a smile graced his lips.

Finally, we allowed the dish to simmer. "Won't take long," I told him. This was the quick version of a tagine.

"That was fun," he admitted. "I should do that more often." *Especially if you get food all over yourself.*

"Not bad, boss," Brian told him. "Never really seen you cook before."

"Thanks. Feels good."

20 minutes later I suggested he add the couscous to the dish. And without thinking, he grabbed the heavy lid without using his towel. "Jesus fucking Christ!" The lid crashed to the

floor and everyone stood still with their eyes on the boss. "Why the hell didn't you tell me it was hot?"

It was something he should have known. Did know but hadn't given it any thought. I grabbed his hand and stuck it under cold running water as he cursed me out. "Was that your idea of a joke? The kitchen's no place for messing around, you fucking idiot." He snatched his hand away and yelled at the staff, "What are you staring at? Get back to work," before storming through the swinging doors.

Fucking idiot! Part of me thought he got what he deserved. But I was overcome with guilt for being pleased he'd gotten burnt. I wished I had someone leading me through this mess. Dad would do that if he were here. He'd know the right thing to do. He'd be able to handle an ass like Larkin.

CHAPTER 8

LARKIN

The sheets were cold when I climbed into bed. And cold again every time I rolled over. This bed was far too big; my body couldn't seem to keep it warm all by myself.

The ghost of a thought whispered through my mind. Bellamy could help me keep it warm…

Gah! That was the whole problem, wasn't it? Bellamy fucking Morley. With his adorable curls and award-winning smile.

And I had gone and made him my prisoner with my deal to pay off his family's debt.

He didn't want to be here. He was only here because I'd left him no other choice. Gods, I hated myself. How could I expect anything other than that same emotion from Bellamy?

I should have just waited for the diner to go belly up. I could have bought the damn thing for a pittance and then bulldozed it, flattened it into the ground so nobody would ever compare my high cuisine to that dollar-store fare again.

I flopped across the mattress again, the cold sheets once more making me swear. "Dammit! Shit! Fuck!" It wasn't the cold sheets pissing me off, not really. And it wasn't even Bellamy or the way he seemed to have this easy friendship with all of my staff. I swore I wasn't jealous of it all, I wasn't!

It was the way Bellamy made me look at myself… I was looking in a mirror, and I didn't like what I saw. I had always ruled my kitchen with an iron fist, fear the biggest motivator to keep everyone in line. And then suddenly Bellamy walked in and everyone was laughing at me. They saw that Bellamy wasn't scared of me, and it was like the magic spell was broken. Who was I now except a mean man, one who couldn't even cook a single dish without burning his hand.

When I rolled over this time, it was straight out of bed. I'd had just about enough of this tossing and turning. Sleep was obviously a pipe dream tonight.

I stormed through the hallway and down the sweeping staircase, slamming my feet onto each stair. My rage had gone from a simmer to a full boil, and nothing would help now except to blow off some steam.

Pots and pans clanged as I tossed them around. Where the hell was the lighter? I hated this stupid gas stove. I just wanted something to be easy, for once. A push of a button, a snap of my fingers.

"Larkin," a soft voice said from behind me, and I swung around, frying pan brandished in front of me.

"Randa," I said, lowering the pan and my voice all in one move. It was hard to yell at my housekeeper. She had a way of narrowing her eyes at me that had me feeling chastised, like a mother would, I suppose, if I still had a mother.

"Would you like me to prepare something for you? A warm glass of milk, perhaps."

I shook my head quickly. "No, thank you. I would much prefer to just be left alone."

"Mm hmm," she sighed, analyzing me. "If you wanted to be left alone, you shouldn't have made it your goal to wake every single person in the household. Jake thought someone had broken in and was trashing the place. He was ready to grab a shotgun and come investigate, but I stopped him. You're welcome."

"Yes. Thank you." Jake was always looking for a reason to bring out the shotgun. He was the gardener, but he fancied himself more of a game warden. I shook my head. "I will try to be quieter."

"Yes, please do."

It wasn't until after she'd left that I realized I should have asked her where the lighter was. "Cold sandwich it is," I muttered to myself. I slapped butter onto some bread and threw a wedge of cheese between the slices. I was about to take a bite when another voice stopped me in my tracks, and this time, it was clearly not Randa.

"Please tell me you're going to fry that."

I turned to find Bellamy standing in my kitchen, his curls deliciously rumpled and wearing nothing more than a pair of pajama pants. I pulled my robe tighter around myself to hide the bulge that was growing at the sight of his chest, his abs, his trail of hair leading down, down...

I gulped and turned away, plopping my sandwich down on the counter. "I'm embarrassed to admit this... but I don't have a clue how to use this stove. My own kitchen, and I'm completely lost."

"So, I guess that's why you made private tutoring as part of our agreement. Let's consider this our first lesson." Bellamy sidled over, nudging me aside. I watched as he turned on the gas and then pressed a button. The stove gave a small click and the gas ignited into a small flame. He adjusted the heat and then moved the pan over top.

"Ah," was all I could say. I was sure if I'd taken a few seconds to think it over, I could've figured it out myself. I could feel my lip sticking out in a pout and sucked it back in before Bellamy could see it. I wasn't thinking clearly, not even a little. Bellamy's scent was strong from this distance, and it was muddling my senses. I shook my head to clear it of the cobwebs. I didn't want him to see me as nothing more than a toddler throwing a tantrum... because I was all too aware that that was exactly what it looked like.

"I'm sorry." Bellamy's words were so quiet that I almost missed them. He simply picked up my sandwich from the counter and buttered the outside, before resting it in the warm frying pan.

"What?" I scoffed, before amending, "I mean, what are you apologizing for? You haven't done anything wrong."

He shrugged, and I tried to ignore the way it made his back muscles bunch and flex. "For teasing you, embarrassing you. My dad would be scolding me so hard for treating you like that."

"Your dad... not the man I met? Not Saul?"

"No, my omega father, Jeremy. He was like a father for all our restaurant staff too. He took each and every one of them under his wing, listened to their troubles, taught them everything he could. And he encouraged them to leave... not in a bad way. I mean, to take their kitchen know-how and to apply to bigger restaurants or to culinary school. And then when they left, he would throw them a huge party. He was the most amazing man." Tears shimmered in his eyes, a contrast to the sweet smile on his lips.

"How did he die?" The words were out before I could stop them, but Bellamy didn't seem to mind the question.

"Cancer." Nothing more needed to be said. Cancer was a bitch. It did its damnedest to break down even the best of us, and even though I had never met Bellamy's dad, I hated to imagine the way cancer had hurt him and his family. I had my own firsthand experience with the way cancer could destroy a family.

I clenched my fists at my side, as though I could fight not just cancer, but time itself, fighting to undo what the past had wrought on poor Bellamy, this gentle omega at my side. He deserved better.

Bellamy scooped the toasted sandwich out of the pan and onto a plate, and then turned off the stove. When he rotated towards me, he was close enough that his chest was nearly brushing against my robe, and I had to fight the urge to move even closer, to feel the heat of his skin against mine.

"So, I'm sorry," he reiterated. When he finally looked up at me, his eyes reflected his regret. "A peace offering?" he asked, raising my plate to me.

"Apology accepted," I said with a slow nod. "But only if you will allow me to apologize in return." He didn't ask why, since it was blatantly obvious to us both that I was an asshole, and one apology wouldn't nearly cover all the things I had to be sorry for. "I don't think making you a sandwich would make up for anything, especially considering I would probably burn it." His smirk was adorable and encouraged me to go on. "I'm not always a nice man, but I'm trying."

Bellamy turned to leave the kitchen, but as he walked away, his fingers brushed over my hand, leaving a trail of fire. "It's a start."

CHAPTER 9

BELLAMY

Monday. The day of rest. The restaurant was closed and I'd slept in late. Glorious sleep. I needed it because most nights since I'd been staying in Larkin's home, I'd tossed and turned until the early hours, usually waking with the sheets in a bunched-up mess and the pillows on the floor.

My dreams had been invaded by monsters. Mythical beasts of every description had tormented me until I shot up in bed, eyes open wide, my body covered in a sheen of sweat.

But today being my day off, I slept the sleep of the dead until late morning. The night before, I'd promised Pop I'd catch up with him after the diner closed, but he refused, saying I needed to rest based on how hard I was working.

Padding along the long hallway, I crept down the stairs. Randa, the housekeeper, wasn't around. She would have offered to make me scrambled eggs if I'd asked but I didn't want to burden her. This house—or to use its correct term, a mansion—was huge. Randa had enough to keep her busy.

Besides, I was a chef and could produce a decent breakfast with my eyes closed and hands tied behind my back. A slight exaggeration perhaps, but I bet I could wield a spatula clamped between my teeth. Hoping to avoid Larkin, I snuck into the kitchen. Though, judging by his lack of knowledge of his own stove, I doubted he was nearby. Probably ate at his club on his days off, if he belonged to one.

Though Larkin had money to buy the best, most luxurious furnishings, the building wasn't a home. There were no cozy nooks with a pile of books beside it. No photos of people laughing on the mantelpiece. No half-eaten packets of cookies in the kitchen. It was more like a museum. On show when the sun was up, but locked away and quiet with no one around after dark.

I wandered out onto the terrace and ate my food, enjoying the warm sunny day and the quiet. No one was saying my name. "What do you think of this, Bellamy?" "Would you taste this, Bellamy?" "This needs something extra, Bellamy."

And then there was Larkin doing his daily storming into the kitchen routine, yelling, "What the fuck is this shit?" as he flung down the day's menu. Trying to make him understand that the menu should change based on what was available was proving to be a grueling lesson. He preferred order, whereas I went with the flow.

Getting up very early before dawn and heading to the markets was part of a chef's life. I'd encouraged Larkin to join me on my morning jaunt, saying it was where I got inspired. What happened to be in the market that day—the freshest ingredients—would determine what would make it onto the diners' plates in the evening. Afterwards, I'd be fired up to create something new and exciting, and eager to get back into the kitchen.

Larkin, on the other hand, started his day either in the office or bellowing at me about a new dish I'd snuck onto the menu. How many more days and weeks left of this?

As I sipped my coffee, I admired Larkin's magnificent garden. It was a riot of color, but much like the inside of the mansion—and the restaurant—it was pristine with not a leaf, petal, or a blade of grass in the wrong place.

I forced myself to go back to the night in the kitchen. The one in the mansion where I made him a sandwich. His iron-clad facade had cracked a little, giving me a glimpse of the man behind the mask. He'd shown a spark of humanity which had me more confused than ever.

I gulped as I recalled my skin brushing against his and hated my body for refusing to listen to my mind. There was no way for my yearning to be anything other than just that. A schoolboy infatuation. And besides, the Larkin that showed himself most of the time was the restaurant owner. Aloof. Bad-tempered. The Larkin who'd apologized rarely made an appearance.

After draining the coffee pot, I got up to stretch my legs and considered taking a nap, even though I'd been awake for less than two hours. I didn't dream during the day. The nightmares only reared their head at night.

As I trudged up the stairs, my gaze rested on a narrow stairway at the end of the corridor. I'd hardly noticed it before, as I came home every night exhausted and stumbled into bed. Also I wanted to barricade myself in my bedroom in case Larkin decided he wanted to chat.

Who was I kidding? Barking, bellowing, shouting, and berating were more his style. Though I did get that one apology from him.

The stairs obviously led to an attic, and I was intrigued. Did he use it as a guest suite? An office? Or was it crammed with junk and memories? With the idea of sleep put on the backburner, I raced up the stairs two at a time and paused at the top.

While it was clean—Randa must mop the room regularly —and there were no cobwebs draped over the windows or a layer of dust on the boxes and furniture, it was obvious this was a neglected part of the house.

I wandered around the room, picking up a book and rose-patterned teacup. There was a pile of what I assumed to be journals in a box. But even though I was snooping in Larkin's attic, I wasn't about to invade his privacy by reading his or someone else's innermost thoughts.

The room had a great view of the garden and driveway leading in from the street. It would make the perfect retreat, as it probably caught the morning sun. I imagined having my morning coffee in this space.

Whoa! Where did that come from? Wherever it was, it could go back to where it came from. I'd be leaving this house after the month was up and didn't plan on returning.

I turned to leave, wanting to get out of the claustrophobic space. But my knee bumped a small open box filled with framed photos. Fascinated, I picked one up.

I sank to the floor as I gazed at what had to be a young Larkin. Maybe four or five, and he was standing between a man and a woman who were each holding one of his hands. *His parents, I assume.* Larkin's mother and father were gazing adoringly at their son and he was obviously basking in their love.

Picking up another photo of Larkin. Older. Maybe in his early teens. Smiling, carefree, his posture relaxed. Others at various stages of his life. Some of him alone. Others with his family. Christmas. Birthdays. And what shone through in each one was love. Larkin himself was almost unrecognizable. Where had that boy gone? Was he buried under the fierce exterior or had that carefree person been banished and ordered never to return?

Why are they here and not on display throughout the house? I heaved myself up. A creak had my head swiveling toward the entrance. "Oh, Jesus! I didn't hear you come up." Larkin was standing at the top of the stairs, veins building on his forehead, while his body hummed with anger and resentment. And then it hit me. He'd caught me snooping among his private possessions. "I'm sorry. I didn't mean to pry."

He strode toward me, nostrils flaring and hands fisted at his sides. "What in the hell do you think you're doing?"

"I just… I…" There was no reasonable excuse for why I was being so nosy. Now it was my turn to apologize. Again. "I really am…"

"Paying your debts, bringing you into my kitchen and my home, does not give you permission to go poking around in my life." His voice rattled the windows and I leaned against an old desk for support.

He outstretched a hand, and it was only then I discovered I was still holding a portrait of him as a young boy. He snatched it out of my hands. "How dare you invade my privacy!" he snarled. He flung the photo in the box, before charging out of the attic. I stayed where I was until he'd clattered down the stairs and the front door slammed.

CHAPTER 10

LARKIN

A beast. That was what I was. I really was a total monster, a boor, a Neanderthal... with the emotional maturity of a fruit fly. Wait, were fruit flies emotionally immature? They must be.

I had spent the better part of the day marching up and down the streets, seeking some kind of validation for the rage still burning in my chest. But instead of finding a reason to keep my temper at a steady roar, I found the rushing pulse retreating from my ears, the red from my vision. With each step, I found myself leaving a droplet of my anger behind, at first a trickle that soon turned into a flood, pouring out of me.

And what was left once the rage was gone?

Bellamy. All that I could see, hear, feel... was Bellamy. The way his face had crumpled when I'd shouted at him, his plea cut short. Why couldn't I just react like a normal man? Somewhere inside, I heard the chiding voice of my father hissing that I wasn't normal, that I wasn't good enough, that everything was my fault. Those pictures that Bellamy found... they were nothing more than a reminder of everything I had lost. Seeing them there, in Bellamy's hand, his eyes all soft… he had no idea the hornet's nest he'd stepped straight into. It wasn't his fault. He hadn't known…

I looked up and found myself right back where I'd started. Home. I scoffed out loud as I thought the word. This wasn't home, not anymore. It had been my childhood home, my mother's… Her will had named me as the benefactor, but besides providing a bed to sleep in, I had no interest in the ghosts held within its walls. Gods only knew why she hadn't left it to my father. The house quickly became a source of disagreement between us, yet another thing for him to blame me for.

I wanted to turn myself off, to forget everything, to just blink and this whole mess would be gone. I had spent so many years boxing up all these emotions, and Bellamy had unpacked it all in less than a month. And just like Pandora's box, shoving everything back in was proving more difficult than I would have imagined. I could send Bellamy straight back to his diner, and he wouldn't mind one bit. He would go back to his job, his father, and I could forget I'd ever laid eyes on the meddlesome omega.

Except…

Even as I tried to convince myself that this was the best course of action, my feet were walking up the front steps. Through the front door, up the main staircase, and down the hall. As I told myself that it would be better to let Bellamy go and close myself back up in my carefully constructed cage, I found myself standing in his bedroom doorway, opening my mouth and saying, "Come with me."

Bellamy looked up at me, his eyes red-rimmed and puffy. I made him cry.

The grief echoed through my hollow shell and rippled, a stone dropped in a pond, rebounding and redoubling on itself.

Our eyes met, and I tried to say everything I couldn't put into words through my gaze. I'm sorry.

I never meant to make you cry.

I'm so lonely it hurts, and you are the only person that makes it feel better.

I didn't know if he understood my unsaid pleas, but he rose up off the bed regardless. He followed me down the hall and up that narrow staircase. The door to the attic was closed; he must have shut it on his way out, and I appreciated the sentiment. But you couldn't close a door on my entire past, it didn't work like that.

The door gave an unholy squeak as I pushed it wide. I noted that the box of pictures was packed back up, tucked under a table, as if that would somehow hide it and everything it represented. I briefly considered pulling out the box, showing each picture to Bellamy, laying my emotions at his feet and leaving myself bare... but no. I'd had enough of flagellating myself today.

No, instead, I turned towards the bookshelf. I reached out for Bellamy's hand to draw him closer, but stopped myself in time, my fingers outstretched. He looked down at my hand, and for a moment we both just stood there staring at it. For one beat of my heart, I wondered if he would close the distance between us and meet me halfway, enclosing his hand over mine. I could almost imagine how soft his skin was, how warm.

I snatched my hand back before he had the chance to react, whichever way he would have gone. Maybe he would have just left me hanging there, waiting... or maybe he would have sneered and slapped my hand away from him. I swept my hand up instead, to the shelves before us.

"Ta-da," I said weakly.

Bellamy raised a brow. "What am I looking at?"

"This... this is my mother's collection. She was the most amazing chef, and these are her recipes." I cleared my throat, trying to clear the lump lodged there. "Help yourself."

Bellamy opened his mouth to answer, but I made to brush past him. I couldn't bear to watch.

His hand on my arm stopped me. "Wait…"

I tilted my head up just enough to peek at him from under my lashes. His cheeks were flushed to a rosy pink; his eyes, though still red from his earlier tears, now shone with a glistening light.

"These books," he said, but the rest of his thought seemed to be overridden with his emotions.

"These were her life's work. You are welcome to go through them, see if there are any secret recipes you can use, combinations of spices or sauces you've never tried. You are also free to use the kitchen. Whatever you need, it's yours."

"Your mother—is she why you decided to invest in restaurants?"

I nodded slowly, my chin dipping down to my chest. "Yes. She loved everything about food—the scents, the flavors—taught me everything I know about cooking."

I could see the look that crossed over Bellamy's face, and I didn't blame him one bit. Everything I knew didn't seem like much. I was clumsy with a knife, burned myself on a pot lid, mispronounced nearly every single foreign dish, and I couldn't even work my own stove. Maybe if my mother'd had more time, I would be a better chef. Maybe if she hadn't died and left me with my father, bitter and spiteful, I would have been more chef than businessman.

I was a disappointment to my mother's memory.

This time, when I moved to leave, Bellamy didn't stop me. Maybe he sensed that I'd reached my limit, that I was teetering on the brink of an emotional meltdown. When I looked back over my shoulder, he was running a finger along the spines of her notebooks, trying to decide where to begin. His excitement lingered on the air, leaving a shiver tickling my skin. An involuntary smile tugged at my lips. My mother would have loved Bellamy.

I was halfway down the attic stairs when his voice called down to me. "You could join me, you know? We could make dinner together. That was the deal, after all."

Did I want to make dinner with Bellamy? My body was in full agreement, and my heart was on board. But my mind… my mind was overwhelmed with grief, guilt, and distrust.

"Maybe next time," I called back, before continuing my retreat.

I sealed myself up in my room for the rest of the night. There was no tossing and turning for me tonight. The bed was warm this time, wrapped as I was in the familiar aromas from the kitchen. Bellamy was cooking… but it was my mother who visited me in my dreams, whispering that she was proud of me.

CHAPTER 11

BELLAMY

It was early afternoon and the lunchtime rush was almost over. One more plate of the special beef bourguignon served to a late-arriving customer and I was done. Though I was constantly updating the menu, the classic French dishes remained, often with a twist instead of the stale old formula, repeated day after day.

I arched my back, worn out after a hectic session in the kitchen, and covered up a yawn. I was free until the evening. It was a good tired. One achieved after being creative and productive and working with a great team.

The staff were incredible, and while we got along well, it was their culinary talent that amazed me every single day. Unleashing their creativity had transformed their work habits and their ideas, and they were constantly pushing the boundaries. The comments from customers, both new and regular, as well as the positive reviews, proved we had given the restaurant a second chance.

I grabbed a bottle of water and headed out the back door. There was a narrow alley behind the restaurant that linked two major roads. At night it was deserted, but now it was bustling with office employees heading back to work after a late lunch.

Sitting on the step and enjoying life passing by was, for me, a great way to unwind.

"Bellamy?" Polly stuck her head out the door. It was unusual for anyone to bother me when I came out here. There was an unspoken rule that this was my quiet time and I shouldn't be disturbed. "There's some guy here to see you. Says he's a friend and wants to get a meal. Keith told him the kitchen had closed except for dessert, but he's being an ass. Said you'd definitely want to see him."

I couldn't imagine any of my friends barging into the restaurant and acting that way. Many had no idea I was here. I'd just said I was helping out a friend for a month and was going to be super busy. Whoever it was had lousy timing, and I'd chew them out for being a butthead and treating the staff badly. We were becoming a family and I looked out for them.

I heaved myself up. "Sorry," Polly said as she went back inside.

After a quick glance at my face in the bottom of a shiny-clean saucepan, I traipsed into the restaurant. At this hour there were only a handful of occupied tables and I spotted him instantly. Also, he was waving a napkin and sort of lunged across the table and proceeded to knock over his water glass. "Bellamy! Finally. I expected you to be greeting customers at the front door."

Not my job. "I'm a chef, Winston," I said through clenched teeth as Keith, the waiter, mopped up the spill.

He pretended to peruse the menu and tossed it on the table. "Why didn't you tell me you were working here now?"

None of your fucking business was what I was temped to say, but I was working and representing Larkin and the restaurant. "The decision was sudden." I glanced around, hoping someone needed me, but was out of luck.

"I was offended you slipped away without a word, and your father refused to tell me where you were."

"It's company policy not to give out employees' personal details." *Fuck the guy and his entitlement.*

"I had to read it on some foodie blog," he spat out as if it was beneath him to search the internet. "And to make matters worse, a waiter told me the kitchen here is closed."

His raised voice got the attention of diners enjoying coffee across the room, and I had to shut him down and get away, if possible. "I believe there's a serving of the beef bourguignon remaining." I sent up a quick prayer hoping I was right.

Dealing with Larkin's tantrums on a daily basis was headache enough, but Winston was a customer and a fuckwit. He wouldn't care about creating a scene, as he neither worked here nor owned the business. "Stay here and I'll check."

"That's okay, I'll come with you. We can spend one-on-one time." He waggled his eyebrows and grabbed his crotch. Oh God, I hated it when guys did that in public!

"Sorry. No can do. Industry regulations." I beckoned the waiter. "But Keith will get you something to drink while you wait." I hurried away without looking back after muttering a brief thanks to Keith.

I didn't have time to make a serving of mashed potatoes, so bread would have to do. Wishing I could hide out in the kitchen, I brought him food along with a smile. "Here you are, Winston." He licked his lips as I placed the dish in front of him. "Enjoy."

"Sit with me, Bellamy." He understood what he was doing, I was sure of it. No way could I brush him off without damaging the restaurant's reputation. He knew it and I knew it. I was officially off duty, so I slumped into a chair opposite him and Keith filled my water glass. "This better be good or I'll have to post a comment on that food blog."

I held my breath as he took a mouthful but needn't have worried. His face transformed from pouty would-be suitor to almost orgasmic. I raised the water glass to put something between him and me. "Wow! This is amazing," he moaned.

"The key is to marinade the meat for a day. Glad you like it." What I didn't tell him was it was Larkin's mom's recipe. It would take weeks to go through her notebooks and read her spidery handwriting. But the first one I'd picked up had been the traditional French recipe but she used ox cheek. It had to be cooked very slowly. But it was worth it.

At the pace he was eating, it'd be dark before I could get rid of him. He curled his lip, making my stomach turn. "And that brings me to my next question. When are we going on a date?" *Never, ever, ever, ever!* He pulled apart a piece of bread and used it to soak up the gravy. *Ewww!* I jumped up and grabbed the bread basket, thankful to have an excuse to leave. "You need more."

"I certainly do." He eyed me up and down. I fled into the kitchen. Some of the staff had left 30 minutes ago, while others were still cleaning up. Joseph was checking the schedule, but I wasn't comfortable asking him to call or interrupt me with a fake excuse. Bringing my personal life into work, despite Winston not being a part of it, wasn't professional.

I dawdled as long as I could before heading back into the dining room. Where was Larkin? I hadn't seen him today, and I wished he'd barge in blustering about something or other and I could make my excuses and disappear.

Winston leaned back and tapped his fingers on the table. "How much longer will we play this game, Bellamy?"

"Game?" I squeaked, thankful we weren't alone.

"You know you want me. And I've been happy to play cat and mouse, but this cat is running out of patience and is ready to pounce." He made a clawing motion and mewed. It was all I could do not to lean over and heave my guts out.

The front door opened and there was no need to turn

around. His scent announced him, and I took a deep breath and inhaled. Winston's gaze was no longer on my face but at a point over my shoulder. Larkin and I didn't know each other well enough for him to recognize a call for help, but I gave it my best shot and turned to face him, my eyes pleaded with him.

"How was lunch?" he asked. I understood he was talking about business, but Winston, being the ass he was, assumed Larkin was speaking to him personally.

"Excellent. My very good friend, Bellamy, knows how to make an alpha drool."

I shuddered as the image his words created burned into my brain.

"As Bellamy's boss, I'm afraid I have to steal him away for a meeting." Oh thank you, someone up there, for answering my prayers.

"No matter. I know here he lives." *What the fuck? How?* The next sentence was directed at me. "I'll call around late tonight with a bottle of something special. It's time." He winked.

Larkin moved behind me, his breath on my neck. The tension between us stretched almost to the breaking point. I cleared my throat. "I'm no longer living at home." It wasn't any of Winston's business where I was laying my head each night, and I definitely wasn't about to tell him, giving him ammunition to needle and stalk me.

Winston's face fell and his eyes darted between Larkin and me. "Lunch is on the house." I caught Keith's eye. "Keith will take care of you if you want a coffee." Turning to Larkin, I said, "Boss, I have to discuss tomorrow's menu," and I stalked into the now-empty kitchen. And he followed me.

CHAPTER 12

LARKIN

*G*ods, I was a fool. But the extent of my idiocy still remained to be seen.

Bellamy stomped ahead of me as I followed him towards my office, through the dining room and into the kitchen. I was scrambling for an excuse for having interrupted him with that... that *alphahole*... but I couldn't help myself. The way he was leering up at Bellamy, as if he had a claim on him. It turned my stomach, had me seeing red. The physical reaction was completely out of left field, nothing I had ever experienced before, but there was no ignoring the urge to separate the two of them.

I gnawed on my lip as I tried to put a name to this emotion. Anger? No, I was far too well acquainted with that emotion, and this was close, but it was also more than that.

I faltered in my steps. Jealousy. There it was. I was jealous. The reality of it made it feel like the floor dropped out from beneath me.

How could I be jealous? That would mean...

I peeked a glance up at Bellamy. His dark eyes, his lean frame... was I attracted to him? Of course, how could I not be, he was a handsome man—but as he looked over his shoulder and our gazes locked, I realized it went beyond attraction.

I was *interested* in him.

"That man..." I began, but I swallowed down the words. What had I been about to ask, exactly? It was no business of mine who Bellamy chose to spend his time with, but on the flip side... for a split second, when I had come up behind him, I had sworn there was a note of panic to Bellamy's voice, a plea for help in his eyes.

I cleared my throat. "I'm sorry for interrupting. If you would like to go back—"

"God! Please, no!" Bellamy interrupted, his raised voice turning heads from the kitchen staff that remained. He seemed to realize his outburst was a bit of an extreme reaction and pulled himself together, lowering his voice to say, "That's all right, thank you anyway. He's... nobody special."

I opened the office door and held it open for Bellamy. He brushed past me, his hip barely grazing against my crotch, and it sent a jolt through me. This was an emotion I was more familiar with. It was a low ache in my gut, the urge to pull him into my arms, throw him across the desk, and bury myself in his ass.

But no. He didn't feel the same way about me. He despised me. And for good reason! I was an asshole!

But maybe I didn't have to be...

I gently closed the door to the office and made my way behind the desk before he could notice the semi I was sporting. I sat, folding my hands across the desk in front of me... and then froze. I had nothing.

"You wanted to have a meeting?" he asked, eyebrow raised.

"Yes, I—" Nope, nothing. "No, actually," I suddenly found myself admitting. "Sorry if I read the situation wrong, I just had a feeling you needed saving." He opened his mouth to speak, but I held my hand up. "Yes, I know, you're a strong, independent omega, and you are perfectly capable of saving yourself."

"No, actually, I appreciate the save," he admitted with a shrug. "Winston is the textbook definition of persistent alpha. He just can't seem to get the hint, no matter how forcefully I say no. If you hadn't interrupted, I likely would've made a scene, so I guess you were doing all of us a favor."

"Oh." I studied his face for signs of his lying, but I should know better than that by now. Bellamy was honest to a fault. Yet another one of his endearing qualities.

We stared at each other across the desk. Neither of us seemed to be ready for this "meeting" to end, but since we didn't have any valid reason for hiding out in here, and there was always plenty of work to do, Bellamy finally pushed his chair back and made to leave.

"Thanks, again… for the save," he said, standing.

He had his hand on the doorknob, when I said, "Wait!" Shit, what the hell was I thinking? He turned around, and the smile playing on his lips had the word launching out of me. "Dinner!"

He turned back to me, his hand still on the knob, and his expression turned coy. "Dinner… prep? You want me to prep for the dinner rush?"

"No, no. I just meant…" Gods, what did I mean? "Maybe I would like to cook something… new for the menu? And maybe you could help me pick one of my mom's recipes to try?"

That wasn't at all what I meant. I had been about to ask Bellamy out for dinner, but that road led only to disappointment and rejection. There was no way that someone as good and kind as Bellamy would ever be interested in a downright beast like me.

"I'd like that," he said softly.

Did he really mean that? Or was he just being the

generous man that I knew him to be, doing me a favor because he didn't want to disappoint me? Was I just another persistent alpha who didn't know how to take a hint?

His grin widened and there was a mischievous glint to his eyes. "Tomorrow," he said simply.

"Tomorrow?" I squeaked, before clearing my throat.

"Yes, tomorrow. You'd better go to bed early tonight, because the market opens before dawn."

"Wait, what?" I spluttered. "What market? Did you say dawn?"

"Mmm," he confirmed, opening the door and stepping out. "We'll need to get you some ingredients for that dinner. Bright and early. I'll drive."

He closed the door behind him, leaving me to my solitude.

Why did I suddenly feel like this dinner was about more than just food? It wasn't a date, obviously. I mean, I would know if I had just asked Bellamy on a date.

Wouldn't I?

CHAPTER 13

BELLAMY

"Remind me again why we're doing this?" Larkin peered at the dark sky that had no hint of the dawn which was still at least an hour away. "It's the middle of the night," he groused. "Torture."

I ignored his complaining and eyed his clothes. It was one of the few times I'd seen him looking less than pristine. A tee and leather jacket hugged his body perfectly, along with rumpled jeans. He had brushed his hair, but the five o'clock shadow that covered his jaw was made for fingers to run through. *Someone else's fingers*, I reminded myself.

We were going to the market in my car. I figured if he was driving, he might put it off or pretend he was sick. Whereas with me in the driver's seat—literally—he couldn't avoid me sitting in the driveway waiting, my hand on the horn, waking up the neighbors and reminding him of his promise to come to the market.

He pulled at the passenger door handle and it came off in his hand. "What the fuck? Is this thing safe?" He peered through the window and mumbled, "It should be condemned."

"Stop it. She'll hear you." I'd been prepared for his

grumpiness and I was adept at dealing with my car's quirks. I opened the door from the inside.

"She?"

"Gouda."

"You named your car after a type of cheese?"

"Why not?" I patted the seat and he gingerly sat down. "Get in or we'll be late and all the good stuff will be gone."

He gave me an *aha* look and went to get out. "In that case, I think I left something in the house…"

I ignored him. "Buckle up," Gouda rumbled and spluttered, and we roared down the driveway. Larkin gripped the seatbelt with one hand and rested the other on the dashboard. His feet hit the imaginary brakes whenever we reached a corner.

"You do have a license to drive this clunker, right?"

"No, I just got up one day and decided I wanted to get behind the wheel. Learned by trial and error." He shot me a terrified look while his mouth was frozen in a silent scream. *Gotcha!* "Here we are," I announced as we tore into the market parking lot and I screeched to a halt.

I got out and picked up two chunks of wood near the far wall and placed them behind a front and back wheel. "Don't ask," I said and strode toward the huge building that reminded me of an airplane hangar.

The market was humming, despite the early hour, and the bright fluorescent lights had Larkin blinking. Now I could see him properly. The jacket made him appear as if he were in a biker gang, a real bad boy. I was tempted to run my hands over the leather and inhale its history, giving me an insight into this alpha who did all he could to push people away. And yet… and yet…

"Bellamy. Over here." Jack, who imported fruit from all over the world, interrupted my thoughts and beckoned me toward open boxes on display at the front of his stall. He held an orangey-pink kidney-shaped object.

"Oh my God, that's amazing." I gave it a sniff. "Pure ambrosia. Larkin, smell this."

He pushed my hand away and screwed up his nose. "Mango? No good for the restaurant. Too stringy."

Jack rolled his eyes and served another restaurateur as I explained, "Not this variety. I agree, some are, and I have memories of sitting in the backyard as a kid with orange strings stuck between my teeth and juice covering my chin."

I couldn't decipher his expression, unable to decide if it was pity or envy.

"Give it a sniff." I outstretched my hand, shoving it under his nose. "Go on." He did as I ordered. "Now I want you to close your eyes and do it again. And tell me what it reminds you of."

"I'm in no mood for kindergarten games, Bellamy." Though he didn't stamp his feet, I imagined that was what he was doing in his head.

"You agreed to come today and this is my domain, so please. Humor me."

"Very well." And I waited as the bad-tempered face was replaced by a more mellow expression. He took repeated sniffs, removed the mango from my hand and cradled it in his. "A beach. Palm trees swaying in the background, and I'm lying on the sand with a book shaded by an umbrella." He pried open his eyes, almost as if he didn't want to leave that beach.

"Would you like a taste?" I asked as I took the mango from his grasp. My fingers brushed over his, which had me wishing I was on that beach with him. He bore a deer-in-the-headlights look, so I clarified, "Of the mango."

"Okay," he croaked and cleared his throat.

Jack expertly sliced the fruit and cut it into cubes. Using a toothpick, I placed one piece on my tongue and handed Larkin the plate. "No strings attached," I snarked.

He studied me with a piercing scrutiny before replying,

"You're not the same Bellamy early in the morning," as he popped the fruit in his mouth.

"Better or worse?" I blurted out, daring him to answer. But he was concentrating on the mango, and I forced myself to watch the range of emotions dancing over his face. If I had to guess, one was bliss.

"What can we make with mango?" he asked as he popped another piece between his lips.

Oh to be that bit of mango. I composed myself and shrugged. "In a salsa, salad, or a dipping sauce with mustard. It goes well with snapper."

"You decide."

"Keep the plate," Jack said when Larkin was obviously reluctant to give it back, and I didn't bother to point out there was a mango stain streak on his t-shirt.

We wandered along the aisles as I examined plump ripe tomatoes. "Let me," Larkin squealed as he inhaled the aroma and the stallholders gave him a taste. It was almost as though he was experiencing a second childhood. He was practically skipping.

To distract myself from the orgasmic look on his face, I picked up a peach. Probably the wrong thing to do. As kids, me and my friends had taken pics of peaches and pretended they were bare bottoms. I ran my finger along the crease and idly wondered about Larkin's ass and if it was as soft as the fruit clutched in my hand.

A timid voice murmured, "Oh my gods," but when I shot him a glance, he twisted away and was looking at a bunch of red grapes. "So expensive."

"Mmmm." Was I imagining he was reacting to me or was it wishful thinking? But I had to stuff my desire back in the bottle and put a stopper in the top.

We continued along the rows of stalls, him tasting everything, me trailing behind, wishing I hadn't asked him to come. The experience had shown me what I couldn't have.

Forbidden fruit! And the longing inside me would have to find another outlet. Perhaps I could take up boxing.

"Heaven," Larkin announced, his sly glance directed at me as he bit into a strawberry.

On the way out of the market, Larkin gushed about the joys of discovering new foods. But as soon as we were alone in the parking lot, he made a face at the stain on his shirt and reverted to his gruff self.

"I'll make my own way home, Bellamy. I can't stomach another ride in Gouda."

CHAPTER 14

LARKIN

"You'll never get Bellamy's attention dressed like that," Randa said.

I startled and looked up, meeting her eyes in the mirror. "What makes you think I want to get Bellamy's attention?"

She gave me a sly look that said I wasn't fooling anyone. I sighed and tried to center myself, find a balance to all the swirling emotions inside me. I used to be so calm… I used to know exactly what I wanted and how to get it… and then in walked Bellamy Morley. Adorable and sweet, thoughtful and considerate. And entirely wrong for me.

"Bah!" I tugged off the tie I had been threading under my collar and tossed it back onto the dresser. "He's not interested in me anyway. He has that alphahole sniffing around him. Bellamy told me he wasn't interested in the guy, but why the hell would he want me? It would just be trading one jerk for another! What the hell does it matter if I wear a blue tie or a red?"

Randa issued one of her patient mom sighs and crossed into my bedroom towards the closet. This room was typically my domain, and other than to give it an occasional dust,

Randa rarely encroached on my boundaries. She didn't look uncomfortable, however, as she swung open my closet doors and started rummaging through my clothes. "I rather think that Bellamy is quite a man apart… wouldn't you agree?"

She wasn't wrong. I gave a slow nod to acknowledge, and she slid the hangers along the track to get right to the back of the closet. "Then, I think," she muttered, her voice muffled from all the suits, "you may need a different approach. Set yourself apart. Yes?"

My breath caught in my throat as I saw the outfit she drew out. "Randa, I don't think I can do this."

"Psh. Of course you can. It's time."

The chef's whites were still creased, unblemished, never once worn. I could just see my name embroidered over the front pocket as Randa slid the outfit off the hanger. "I'll give them a wash for you, get out that stale closet smell."

"Randa, no. They won't even fit properly." I patted my stomach as if I had a beer gut, though in fact, I was probably in even better shape than I'd been when my mother had gifted me those whites, well over a decade ago.

I had still been a fresh-faced teenager then, with hopes of following in her footsteps. She'd bought them a bit on the large side for me then. She had teased, "They're wearing them big these days," but in fact she had purchased them too large intentionally, giving me room to grow into them. I wasn't a chef as it was, so it wouldn't have been proper for me to wear them anyway.

I tried to stop Randa on her way out of my room. "Wait, no, Randa! I'm not even a chef! It isn't right."

But there was no stopping this woman on a mission. "You own that kitchen, Larkin. Now act like it."

∼

I couldn't meet anyone's eyes as I came in the back door of the restaurant that evening. I didn't want to see their judging looks as I came in. Sure, I may have been their boss, so they probably wouldn't say anything against me outright, but ever since Bellamy had set foot in this restaurant, everything had changed. The atmosphere in the kitchen had gone from cold and efficient, to warm... and even more efficient.

As hard as it was to admit that I was wrong, Bellamy had shown me that fear and anger was obviously not the best approach to running a business. It wasn't working for me. Now, the food was more delicious, ethnically diverse and vibrant, the customers had started raving about the changes being made, and the food critics were agreeing. I may have even heard a rumor that Maria Tristov was reconsidering returning to sample the menu again, to give us another shot.

The din in the kitchen tapered off, like a held breath, and I slowly brought my eyes up. Joseph caught my gaze and held it, offering a small smile. "Looking good, sir," he said.

"Hear hear!" Polly called from the back, raising a wooden spoon above her head.

"I didn't want—" I began, clearing my throat before explaining, "I'm not a chef. I know you have all worked hard to earn your positions here, and you continuously amaze me with your talent. I haven't earned these." I gestured down to my crisp whites.

Michael stepped over and placed a hand gently on my shoulder. "Then it's time we put you to work, don't you think? We'll make sure you feel like you've earned them. Deal?"

"Deal," I agreed. I shrugged off my coat and threw it on a hook and then got straight to work. I scanned the kitchen for Bellamy, but he was nowhere to be seen.

Brian must have seen something on my face because he

leaned in and whispered, "He's had to go pick up some special ingredients for tomorrow's special. He'll be back to help us close up."

"Oh. Yeah. Of course." Disappointment skittered through me.

Brian put me to work kneading dough. "Best to do this stuff while you're still nice and clean," he said. "Give it time, and that nice clean coat will be covered in stains. Consider it a rite of passage."

I tried to tell myself that I hadn't gotten dressed up for nothing, but it turned out that Brian had been very right. As I moved onto the soup and it splattered down my chef's coat for the first time, I sighed. I had hoped Bellamy would see me with the outfit unstained. Now I was going to look a total mess when he came in.

Next, Polly had me chopping mushrooms. I had to leave my ego at the door for this, as it was almost like I was starting over from scratch. My prep cook was offering me lessons on how to hold the damn knife, how to avoid chopping off the tips of my fingers. "We don't want blood to stain that nice coat of yours," she said with a wink.

Charlie had me make a roux and Michael taught me to sear meat. By the end of the evening, I had worked through all the stations. I was blown away with everyone's patience. My heart swelled as I truly began to feel like this was my kitchen, and they had all helped me to be more comfortable with the tools, with the heat and the bustle, the camaraderie.

I smiled softly to myself... that was, until I glanced at the clock. "We closed 20 minutes ago!" I blurted. "Why the hell are we still cooking?"

Joseph sidled up to me and took me by the elbow. I allowed myself to be tugged over to the side, where there were two dishes laid out on the counter. "I think you should take this out to the dining room. It's time for you to enjoy your reward. You worked hard on this meal, you've earned it."

I looked down, and sure enough, it was a collection of all the foods I had prepared. The mushrooms I had chopped, the roux turned into a sauce for the steak I had seared. Joseph didn't say anything else, just took a step back and melted away into the background. I turned around to take in the rest of the staff, and I was rewarded with winks and smiles as they turned off the grill and began to clean their stations.

"But there are two plates…" I began, but as no one had anything to say, I picked up the plates and stepped through the swinging doors to the dining room.

The lights had been dimmed, making the candlelight's warm glow the primary focus. One table, right in the middle. "Bellamy?"

"There you are!" he said, his smile beaming. "Joseph promised me you had prepared the most amazing meal."

I practically floated across the room, that was how light I felt. I placed the dishes on the table and lowered myself into my chair across from Bellamy, barely aware of Keith appearing to pour us each a glass of wine.

"Well, aren't these guys just the slyest bunch you've ever met? I had no idea I was cooking for you."

His expression fell the tiniest bit. "Oh… is that a problem?"

"No!" I gasped. "Not at all. It's just, if I'd known, I would have been more precise." And then I giggled, legit giggled like a schoolboy. "Honestly, if I'd known, I probably would've been too nervous and burned the whole thing into a charred mess."

Bellamy's shoulders relaxed and he laughed, the most beautiful sound I'd ever heard. Had I ever made him laugh before? I made a mental note to be sure to make him laugh every single day.

I shoved down the thought about our impending deadline. Bellamy would only be here for another week, and then he would be free to return to his old life. He never had to see me again if he didn't want to.

But what if he wanted to…?

I fell into his gaze. "What's the gray stuff?" he asked.

"It's a mushroom pate." I went on to explain all the dishes I had helped put together, and then I had the absolute joy of watching him put each into his mouth, listen to the sounds he made.

It was the single most erotic experience of my life.

"Everything is so delicious," he moaned, and when I mirrored his moan, but for an entirely different reason, his eyes darted up to mine, his pupils dilating.

"Everyone has gone home," he whispered, and I became suddenly aware of how quiet and still the restaurant had become.

"So it seems." Was he implying we should leave? Even though I would be taking him home, I wasn't ready for this evening to end. I didn't want us to disappear into our separate rooms for a night alone.

I set my napkin aside and prepared to push my chair back from the table, but Bellamy reached out and grabbed my hand. His skin was warm, almost flushed, and when I looked up, I saw that his cheeks matched. "Don't go," he said softly, but there was an edge to his voice.

"We're done eating," I said cautiously. "And we are the last ones here. Why should we stay?" I said it as an invitation, and I was glad to see he took it that way.

He rose from his chair and walked around the small table. I rotated in my seat so I could face him. Bellamy nudged my legs with his knee so that I parted them, allowing him to move between them, to get closer. Without thought, my hands came up to settle on his hips, and I gave a gentle squeeze, both a reminder to myself that I didn't want to push him too far too fast, as well as conveying a message to him, that if he wanted me, I would meet him halfway.

"Your jacket is stained." Those were not the words I had expected from him. "You should take it off. You need to soak it so it doesn't get ruined."

Oh. Ohhhh! "Yeah, you're absolutely right." He moved back so I could stand before him, and then, with fumbling fingers, he helped me unbutton the jacket and slide it over my shoulders.

The air from the restaurant was cool against my skin, but the brush of Bellamy's breath was enough to have me feverish. I reached down to the table and dipped a finger in the leftover sauce. "Oops," I said, smearing it on Bellamy's shirt. "You'd better soak your shirt too."

The last clear thought I had was the thrum of lust from Bellamy's smile, his dark eyes glittering, and then he leaned over and blew out the candle. We were thrown into veritable darkness, using our hands to feel our way. His lips on mine tasted of the sour wine, but as I worked my way down his throat, to the planes of his chest and then lower, it was as if he tasted sweeter the further I got.

Clothing was discarded and dishes smashed as we cleared the table. I threw him back against the table, and we both held our breaths, hoping it could hold our weight.

"Larkin," he groaned as I hovered above him. Our cocks rubbed together with a delicious friction, but there was only one thing we both wanted in this moment. "I need you."

I reached down to find his entrance drenched with slick. "Oh Bellamy, gods, you're so wet." I probed his hole with a finger, testing, teasing, stretching as I added a second finger, then a third.

"We'll have time for foreplay next time," he panted, his fingers digging into shoulders. "Fuck me, Larkin. Fuck me now!" I wished I could see his face as he promised me a next time. Did he mean it? I was about ready to pull out my day planner and book in a session with him every day from now until eternity.

I lined myself up and pushed forward just enough that the head of my cock was inside him. I paused, just for one brief moment, trying to memorize the feel of him beneath me, the scent, his taste as I leaned in and claimed his mouth with mine.

And then I thrust in, fully sheathed in his channel, and I could no longer see the details. I was overwhelmed by it all, my senses on overload. We moved together as if we were made for each other; Bellamy was everything I had ever wanted, and yet never dared to hope for.

"Bel, my knot—" I warned.

"Yes, Larkin, give me your knot. Fill me, yes, yes—" He gripped me tightly, and I could feel his body tightening like a coiled spring. He threw his head back, his fingers gouging, clawing. He was so close.

I increased my speed, holding his hips steady as the table creaked beneath us. "Come for me, Bel."

I held back my orgasm as long as I could. "Shit!" Bellamy huffed out, his cum spurting from his cock to coat us, and with a final thrust, I released myself into his ass. My knot expanding, filling him and locking us together.

I collapsed against him, panting. "Wow," I whispered.

"Yeah… wow," Bellamy agreed, his fingers tracing lines against my skin.

No other words were needed.

CHAPTER 15

BELLAMY

*T*he morning after. After sex.

I could divide my relationship with Larkin into pre- and post-sex. Pre-sex was prickly, with me wanting to escape and alternately needing to be closer to him. Imagining me in his embrace and then hating myself for wanting that beast of a man! There'd been tears, curses, and nightmares, but on the flip side, the alpha's presence stoked a fire inside me.

But now we were in the post-sex period. Sleeping together changed everything. Wait, who was I kidding? There'd been no sleeping on that table. Just hard, fast, and rapturous sex. The man knew what to do with his cock!

Wishing I could stay in bed and eat a leisurely breakfast on the terrace, I jumped in the shower, grumbling about having to get to the market before the sun came up. Though I'd showered last night when I got home, my clothes were where I'd tossed them—on the floor—and Larkin's scent permeated the bathroom.

Inhaling that aroma that I swore was still on my skin had my thoughts returning to the previous evening when the dishes crashed to the floor. And as well as the aroma of sex, memories of Larkin's cock buried deep inside me would always be accompanied by the fragrance of the roses from the center of the table that ended up scattered on the floor in amongst pieces of broken crockery and water pooled on the hardwood floor.

After getting dressed, we'd cleaned up the mess, hardly saying a word. I was lost in my own thoughts, as I assumed Larkin was. We swept and mopped and rid the restaurant of any sign of our fucking. Hot, sweaty, rip-your-clothes-off passionate fucking. Images kept flashing in my head because it had been so perfect.

And when we were done, I'd stalled my departure by pretending to check things in the kitchen, not wanting to be the first to leave. What was that? A one-off? Did it mean more to me because I initiated it? What did you say to your boss/life-savior who threw you over a table and fucked you? And I was staying in his house which made it more awkward.

So I did what I'd done every night. Picked up my keys and said I was headed home. He had his own car. It was weird because he'd been inside me not an hour before and had his mouth on me. And yet we parted as friendly colleagues.

I'd considered crawling in Larkin's bed for the night, but he didn't invite me. If what we'd done was a one-off, I wouldn't have been welcome.

I fell into bed which was my usual routine after a long day at work. But I tossed and turned as Larkin inhabited my dreams. He'd pushed out the monsters that came to me every night when I closed my eyes. But it wasn't the Larkin who'd fucked me. It was the other one. The damaged, shouty one who constantly lost his temper and rubbed against life like sandpaper on wood.

And now I was in the alley behind the restaurant, ready to begin work. For the first time since the day I stepped foot into Larkin's kitchen, my damp palms revealed how nervous I was. Would the staff sense what had happened between us?

Had Joseph inspected the garbage bins, discovered the broken plates, and he'd be sporting a smirk when I arrived?

"Bellamy?" Brian walked past me as he headed inside. "You okay?" He grinned. "You know the kitchen is inside, right?"

I brushed a hand over my face. "Yeah. Just thinking about… never mind." He gave me an odd look, and I followed him into the building. But with the night's memories fresh in my head, I was worried I'd give away Larkin's and my secret.

But other than greeting me in the usual way, no one acted differently. The tension I'd been carrying seeped away and I got on with my chores. I'd made it over the first hurdle. The second was more problematic. Larkin. Meeting him had different scenarios swirling in my head. He might never speak to me again. Or perhaps he'd be embarrassed at what we'd shared. The third option was the scariest. What if he wanted more? It wasn't something I'd considered.

"How was last night?" Polly asked.

Oh God, she knows. They all do. "Last night?" I croaked.

"Yeah, the dinner that the boss cooked."

"Right," I gulped. "The food. Amazing. Larkin really outdid himself."

"Great." She hesitated as if expecting me to spill more details, but that wasn't happening, even though Polly was probably the one person I'd confide in if I was going to share.

I heard his voice before he barged into the kitchen. He was grumbling at Joseph about something I couldn't quite hear. And when the doors swung open, I busied myself at the stove, not wanting to catch his eye.

I couldn't bear to see regret. Or would it be something else? As we had both shied away from discussing it last night, I couldn't be certain. Heck, I'd never be sure of anything with Larkin. My emotions were teetering on a knife's edge and my hands were trembling as I chopped onions and carrots.

"Today's menu looks interesting. I can't pronounce half

the names but I'm sure someone can fill me in." Did he really say that? Perhaps the real Larkin, the grumpy, blustery one, had been abducted by aliens. Surely it couldn't be because he'd... we'd... had sex.

The word 'fill' had me pause. He'd more than filled me last night. Stuffed his cock in my channel and made mincemeat of my emotions. Despite the heat in the kitchen, goosebumps crawled over my flesh and I rubbed the back of my neck. I stifled a gasp as I tossed ingredients in the pan, but apart from the sizzle of heat searing the vegetables, the room was dead quiet.

Larkin cleared his throat. *Don't make me look around. Not with everyone here.* Eyes were fixed on my back, I just knew it. Waiting for me to respond. There was no putting it off. I glanced over my shoulder. *Yikes!* They really were staring at me, Larkin in particular. His fingers clutching the menu were twisting the paper and tearing the edges.

I finally got up the courage to look at his face, and the uncertainty I felt was mirrored in his eyes. He was leaning slightly forward as if ready to hang on whatever I said. His broad shoulders were hunched and the poor menu hadn't survived his assault. I had my answer.

This was Larkin's way of sending a message, and assuming I'd translated it correctly and hadn't gotten the signal confused, he'd made his intention obvious with that vague question—at least in the short term, although the distant future was still unclear—and it was up to me to give an answer.

Why couldn't he be like most people and invite me to the movies or hold my hand or say something nice? Here we were surrounded by other people, and I put my weight on one foot and then the other, trying to delay the inevitable. "Bellamy!" Polly shouted.

"What? Huh?" *Oh shit!* The unmistakable aroma of burning onions finally penetrated my brain that Larkin and his question had turned to mush. "Sorry. Sorry." Thank God I hadn't ruined a batch of fillet steak. "I didn't get much sleep last night." Why the fuck did I say that?

"I'm waiting," Larkin said, his voice breaking a little. I had to put him out of his misery, but I was so distracted, I made the same mistake he had made the night we'd cooked the tagine. I grabbed the pan handle without using my towel. "Goddammit!" I yelled.

"It's okay, I've got this." Larkin shoved my hand under the faucet and my mind bounced between the pain from the burn and pleasure at having him holding me. Again.

"I'm surprised, a seasoned professional like yourself making a mistake like that."

"I was distracted." I lowered my voice. "It was your fault." He smirked, and I wished we were alone as we had been last night.

"I know just the place to recover."

"I don't need to go to the hospital," I told him. "It's not that bad. "

Tucking his arm in mine, he dragged me toward the walk-in freezer. "What are you doing?" I hissed.

"Kissing you," Larkin whispered as he pulled the door shut. Avoiding my sore hand, he placed his lips on mine and I shivered. But not from the cold. His presence made me jelly. He sucked my bottom lip as one hand brushed over my ass.

"Last night," I mumbled through his kiss. "It was…" But his tongue begging to be allowed into my mouth cut off the words.

"Mmmm," he whispered. "It was."

I pulled away. "How did you know what I was going to say?"

He nuzzled my throat and grunted against my skin, "It was you who yelled, 'Fuck me now' and 'Wow,' wasn't it?" His fingers cupped my growing arousal.

"Maybe," I grinned and kissed the tip of his nose. "But we

need to get back out there. The staff will be wondering what we're doing." And then I joked, "Unless you bring everyone in here for some afternoon delight."

The smile was wiped from his face. Fuck, I said the wrong thing. "Joke. It was a joke. A bad one, obviously."

"You're the first person in a long time that has made me feel anything, Bellamy."

"In that case, perhaps you could kiss me again."

"I could." He gave me a quick peck on the lips. "But I was thinking of using my mouth for… other purposes."

"*What?*" *Oh my God, a blow job in the restaurant freezer.* Steamy, sizzling hot meets ice-cold. Larkin didn't wait for my response. While he smirked and stared into my eyes, his hands worked overtime. I gulped as my pants puddled at my feet. Seconds later, my briefs had been yanked down and my cock, which was swelling, was exposed to the low temperature. I shivered as the air kissed my bare skin.

"You're freezing," he muttered as his lips sucked at my shoulder and his fingers fondled my cock. "I'll have to fix that." He squatted at my feet and rubbed his chin over the tip of my dick before tracing the head over his lips.

Desire had my eyelids close. Shutting down one sense so the others could experience the sensations that were choking me. Warm breath billowed over my length as his hand cradled my balls. "Larkin…" No words could express what I was feeling.

I pushed my hips forward and a warm, wet tongue licked over one side of the shaft and back to the head. It circled the end, lapping at the drops of pre-cum I was certain teetered at the tip.

My imagination could not have prepared me for the way my body stirred, and I reached out in the darkness and grabbed a tuft of Larkin's hair as his lips slid over my cock. He swallowed me, and my body spasmed while being buffeted by wave after wave of desire.

In the back of my mind, I pictured the staff outside, maybe sniggering and giving one another all-knowing glances. But also perhaps checking the time because they needed to get something from the freezer. Maybe Larkin had the same idea, because he gripped my cock at the base and sucked back and forth. Mouth and hand in tandem.

"Jesus Christ, that's good," I moaned as his other hand moved from my balls to my ass, drenched in slick. He wasted no time and one finger plunged into my hole. My body twitched with the two-pronged assault, and I raked my nails over his scalp, his groans mingled with mine.

And then he took it to the next level. He hummed, and the vibrations sent lust pulsing through my veins as I purred, and my body and mind no longer registered the cold. Only heat. And passion.

Arching my back and whimpering, I moved against his mouth as his teeth grazed my shaft. I couldn't hold on any longer. Didn't want to. I needed to experience the pleasure and gave in. My body trembled as fireworks filled my head and I exploded in Larkin's mouth.

He waited until I stopped trembling, and because my body was jelly, he helped me get dressed. When we walked outside, he announced, "I believe those sausages will be perfect, Bellamy. Thank you for pointing them out. I can almost taste them."

I hate him! I lowered my eyes and stalked back to my station, secretly hoping I could come up with an excuse to go another round.

CHAPTER 16

LARKIN

*M*y eyes couldn't stop trailing after Bellamy. Not as he flipped and sauteed, not as he licked the spoon, his tongue trailing along the utensil's edge in the most sensual way. And certainly not when he kneaded the pastry into submission, his hands squeezing, massaging the dough.

Yeah, I was essentially hard the entire day.

Once or twice I caught Joseph's knowing glance. He was onto us, no doubt, but what exactly was he thinking? I wasn't even sure what to think. I mean, obviously there was something between us, but that wasn't how things had started out in the first place. He was only here because I had forced him into this position. Hardly sounded romantic.

Oh gods, I was paying him to be here. Was this like prostitution? Shit.

Now my stomach plummeted straight down to my feet. This was like some kind of roller coaster. Bellamy's eyes were full of heat when he looked up, and it eased a bit of my anxiety, but how could I know for sure? I didn't exactly have a lot of experience in the love department.

Did I say love? No, obviously not. It was far too soon to

be throwing the L word around. Dating, that was what we were doing. Not even that! Fucking! Yeah, that. Hot, pounding sex, and we'd only done it the one time, plus that blowjob. But I had hopes of a repeat performance…

If… If Bellamy wanted it too, that is. His lips in the walk-in freezer had certainly felt like he did, his cock in my mouth, his cum against my tongue, but…

I couldn't stand to be in this kitchen for a moment longer. I was slowly going crazy with the churning doubt and lust, pushing and pulling me in all directions. Bel and I needed to talk this out, but the restaurant was far too busy to catch even a five-minute break.

"Joseph, the kitchen is yours. I'm going to walk the dining room," I barked, and his eyes widened at my sharp tone. "Sorry," I tacked on as I whisked past and through the swinging doors. "Haven't been sleeping well."

"That makes two of you," he muttered. I glanced back once just as the doors swung shut behind me and caught a brief glimpse of Bellamy, the dark circles under his eyes. So, he hadn't slept well last night either. Was it because we hadn't talked over what the sex meant? Or was it because he'd only had sex with me out of some kind of financial obligation?

I ran a hand down my face, wiping away the stress, for a few minutes at least. This was what I was good at. I may not have inherited my mother's talent in the kitchen, but after she died, my father had made damn sure that I could manage a business as well as he did.

I plastered on the signature charismatic smile and prepared to woo the customers. I approached the first table, introduced myself, asked if they were enjoying their meal or if I could do anything to make their experience memorable. Then on to the next table, shaking hands, greeting diners. All smiles, every one of them beyond impressed with the whole experience.

As I wound my way through the sea of tables, I made note that this was no longer the restaurant it had been a month ago. What had once been crisp and white, sterile and bland, was now bursting with color and laughter. All of this was thanks to Bellamy. He had breathed life into not just the restaurant… but into me as well.

I panned my gaze across the crowd and then stopped suddenly, my eyes snagging on a familiar face. He wasn't smiling, not even a little. In fact, he was scowling, his eyes trained directly on me.

It was the alphahole who'd been dining with Bellamy the other day. William? Werner? Something like that.

The businessman in me suggested that I walk away, send Joseph to tend to the grouchy customer since he obviously had a beef with me. But the alpha in me reared its head. There was no way I was going to walk away from what was clearly a challenge from the man.

I swooped through the room and descended on the table, glad to have the upper hand, standing above him and forcing him to crane his neck to look up at me.

"Ah, so good to see you again. Wendell, was it?"

"Winston," he growled, his lip curling into a sneer. Testosterone was coming off him in waves, and I had to fight myself not to take a step back from the godawful stink.

"Right. Winston. And to what do we owe the pleasure of your visit? Here for lunch?" I made note of the empty table in front of him, the menu left discarded to the side.

"I seem to have lost my appetite," he growled.

"That's unfortunate." What else was I supposed to say? If he thought I was going to offer him another meal on the house, he would find himself sadly mistaken. The last thing I needed was a freeloader who thought he could just keep coming here and mistreating my staff, eating my food without paying a dime.

"You see," he began to say, and then seemed to reconsider

his position and rose to his feet so he could attempt to look me in the eye. Too bad he came up a few inches shorter than I was. I made sure to angle my head in such a way that I was still looking down my nose at him. "You see," he started again, breathing his putrid breath in my face, "I can smell him on you. On your clothes. You've had your hands on my omega."

That roller coaster in my gut took another plunge. I did my best to school my features, to keep the surprise from registering, but something must have shown because Winston gave a slow predatory smile.

"Yeah, that's right," he said. "He's mine. And you would do well to keep your hands to yourself if you don't want me to shove my fist through your teeth."

I could feel a few eyes turning our way, customers beginning to take notice of the storm brewing.

"I'm afraid you're mistaken." I had no idea how to defuse this situation. I had rarely been involved in a relationship at all, but now, if what he was saying was true, I was now dangerously close to being a homewrecker. I could feel a cold sweat prickling at my hairline.

If there was one thing my dad taught me, it was how to bullshit a bullshitter. I broadened my grin and reached out to clasp a hand around Winston's in a tight handshake. To anyone observing, it would look like we were the best of friends. What they couldn't see was how tightly my hand was gripping his, the bones grinding beneath my palm. Winston's eyes tightened, but he refused to back down.

He tried to widen his own smile, but it ended up more as a grimace. He leaned in and hissed, "Just back off. He's mine."

I almost didn't let go when he pulled back. I nearly jerked him closer and planted a fist straight onto that dimpled chin of his… but people were watching. So instead of obeying the baser urges of my alpha nature, I gave his hand one last shake and released him.

Winston slunk out the door, shaking out the pain in his right hand. Keith glanced over at me, a questioning glance in his eye. I swore the question was "Do you want me to follow him and teach him some manners?" I gave a small shake of my head and a sad smile, before making my way back to the kitchen.

When I saw Bellamy again, I regarded him in a new light. As someone else's omega.

Maybe the sex last night really hadn't meant anything to him. Maybe it was all part of some kind of obligation he felt to me, for the financial help I had given to him and his father. Maybe he was already in a serious relationship with Winston.

Because why else would an amazing man like Bellamy have anything to do with a beast like me?

The roller coaster wasn't coming back up this time. The ride was officially over.

CHAPTER 17

BELLAMY

Shit. I overslept. Something I never did. But my tossing and turning had continued until the wee small hours, leaving me precious little time to sleep before heading to the market. Larkin and I had not had a serious conversation about... well, about anything other than work, and so sleep still eluded me.

With no time for a shower, I hurled myself into the car and floored it, pleased for once it was not yet light and there were few cars on the road. Normally I loved this time of the morning, when the past's mistakes had been swept away and nothing had yet blotted and stained the new day.

Luckily, my friendship with and being a loyal customer of the market traders had paid off. Assuming I'd been held up, they'd saved me cuts of meat, the freshest of vegetables and fruit, as well as huge shrimps which had just arrived from the coast.

Being late and stressing that I'd be left with what no one else wanted had pushed thoughts of Larkin out of my head. But as I picked up a coffee just outside the market and headed out, he charged back into my mind. Of course he did.

Apart from when I was deeply invested in cooking, there wasn't a moment Larkin wasn't tap dancing around in my thoughts. *Damn that alpha!*

My phone rang but I was driving and couldn't answer. It was in my messenger bag on the passenger seat, and as it continued to ring, my anxiety level increased a notch. *Who's calling me so early in the morning?* It stopped. Thank God! Probably a wrong number. Please let it be.

Memories flooded back of the phone call I got in the middle of the night saying Dad had been taken to the hospital. His finishing chemo had finally allowed us to smile and look forward to the future, but when the cancer returned, he'd been due to start a new round the following week.

He didn't make it.

The phone started up again, its incessant beeping, like a hammer pounding on my brow. I pulled off the road. It was Pop. Thank God. If it had been an unknown number, I would have freaked. "Pop," I said. "Everything okay?" I was almost done with my month at La Belle Compagne, so I'd be home soon.

Instead of his voice wafting through the phone, I winced as a hacking cough greeted me. My heart constricted. "Pop? You okay? What's wrong? Where are you?" A barrage of questions probably wasn't what he needed, but I needed reassurance that this was just a nasty cold. Nothing more.

His labored breathing turned that idea on its head. "Bel," he gasped, and my fingers squeezed the phone as if I was trying to send him my own breath. "I'm… not well." He coughed, and I made a face as I conjured up a vision of him straining to speak. "Pneumonia," he managed to get out.

"Where are you?" If he was in the hospital, the universe was playing a cruel trick. I'd seen this movie and knew how it played out. It was déjà vu at its most vicious. And the smell I associated with hospitals during Dad's stay made me sick to the stomach.

"Home."

"I'm on my way."

Another bout of coughing. "No… the… d-diner." It didn't take a genie to understand making the effort to speak was painful and required all his strength. "D… d… debts."

He sighed, and I jumped in, needing to ease his concerns and not wanting him to waste his breath. "Forget that. It doesn't matter." Pop was all I cared about. We could lose the diner, I didn't care. And if Dad were here, he'd say the same. Pop first and everything else be damned. "I have to make a quick detour and then I'll be home. You okay till then or…?" By asking the question and putting the words out into the universe, it would be impossible to take them back. But I had to know. "…Do you need an ambulance?"

"I'm… fine," he puffed. He obviously wasn't. "Just… just need you."

"I'll be there soon, Pop." I sent him a hug across the city and hoped he got it. I had to tell Larkin, and he deserved to hear what I had to say in person. It could be the last time we saw one another. His anger and disappointment might have him lashing out. But none of that mattered.

My life away from him and the restaurant would be very different going forward. I'd have to get a job in an attempt to make a dent in our remaining debt. Or we'd be faced with selling the diner to get by.

It was early, so Larkin would still be at home, and I roared into the driveway, relieved his car was there. Leaving the engine running and the door open was appropriate because I was closing the door on a future I'd envisioned.

Hurtling into the house, and racing up the stairs two at the time to grab my stuff, I shouted for him, "Larkin! Larkin!" I beat on his door as I passed by, before charging into my own.

He poked his head through the door, and I assumed the urgency in my voice had woken him, as he wore PJ bottoms and his hair was sticking up. "What's happened? The restaurant?"

Poor Larkin that his first thought went to bricks and mortar. He had no close friends and no family. It was all he had. "The staff? Are they all right?" If I hadn't been under so much pressure and worried about Pop, I'd have hugged him. He was a good man under that gruff exterior.

"Bel, tell me, what is it? Are you sick? You don't look sick."

"It's Pop."

His mouth gaped and he made to speak and then obviously thought better of it. I turned away and stuffed clothes in my bag.

His voice, when he eventually found it, faltered. "He's... he's not..."

Swirling around, my nostrils flared as I pummeled his chest. "He's not dead, if that's what you mean. Do not say that word! He's sick, and I have to go to him." Tears streamed over my cheeks. For Pop. And Dad, who would have been making chicken soup for him if he'd been here. For the diner. For what might have been with Larkin.

"I'm sorry," I gulped away the fear that had handcuffed itself to me the moment I heard Pop's frail voice. "Our agreement. I can't complete the contract." My fingers fumbled with the suitcase, and I bent my head, unable to stare into his eyes and witness whatever lay in their depths.

"No," he placed his hand on my shoulders and twisted me around until I was facing him. "I'm the one who should apologize." The cocky alpha, the one who trumpeted his insecurity and frustration with arrogance, was replaced with a man who had an air of resignation, based on his hunched shoulders and his quivering bottom lip.

Wishing I could soothe away his sadness, I squeezed his hand. I had nothing to offer him. My past was dictated by loss. And now my future may follow the same path. Loss of work, friendship, and something that had never been expressed and now never would.

"I should have never dictated the terms of our agreement as I did. I took away your freedom."

"It's…"

"There's no need to say anything. I'm giving it back. The hours you spent creating new dishes, encouraging the staff to find something inside them that they didn't know they had. The camaraderie you built and your ability to use food to bring people together have far surpassed what I expected. I am forever in your debt. You've done everything and more than I ever expected. I will honor my part of the deal. The remaining payment will be deposited into your account today."

"But I…" He silenced me with a finger on the lips. *Is this how we end? With so many things left unsaid?* Perhaps it was appropriate, as whatever we had been was characterized by both of us avoiding and hiding the truth. Our relationship had reached a dead end, and I had to reverse course.

"Larkin, I…" The phone buzzed. "Yes, Pop. I'm on my way." It wasn't Pop. No, I screamed inwardly. This can't happen again. I'd lost one parent, I couldn't lose a second.

"Bellamy? It's Danny."

"Where's Pop?" I yelled as fear crept over my body and had me pulling the shirt away from my throat and clawing at my skin.

"He's right here. I just wanted to make sure he'd called you."

"I'm coming."

"Go," Larkin said as I tossed the phone in my bag. "And don't worry about the diner. It's safe. Concentrate on your father."

"Thank you," I mumbled. "I'll never forget what you did for us."

He waved his hand. "Compared to what you did for me, it was nothing. Now, go." He removed his hand from my elbow, and I gave a feeble wave as I hurried down the stairs and out of his life.

CHAPTER 18

LARKIN

"Sir?"

I looked up at Joseph. It was clear from his expression that this wasn't the first time he had tried to get my attention. "Sorry, what?"

"I was just saying that it smells delicious." He gave me a soft smile, and I had to turn away. I couldn't stand the pity that laced that look. They all looked at me that same way. With pity and regret. Gods, I hated that.

"Thanks," I muttered and turned back to the stove.

I went back to my stirring, but I could still feel him there at my back. I refused to look, to ask him what else he wanted. I had no interest in what he had to say.

Polly piped up from her station, shouting loud enough to be heard over all the bubbling and sizzling and the general kitchen hubbub. "Boss, I think what Joseph meant to say was that you shouldn't have let him go."

I whirled on them. "And what the hell else was I supposed to do?! Keep him here while his father was possibly dying? What kind of a monster do you take me for?"

All eyes turned to me, and I was bombarded with a wave of shame. Mixed with the grief, and all these emotions were nearly enough to drown me. I moved back to the pot in front of me and dipped in a spoon, tasting the concoction. Ahhh, delicious. If I could just focus on the food, everything would be all right. I wouldn't think about how I hadn't heard from Bellamy in over a week. I could ignore the fact that I refused to wash his scent from his bedsheets, but still, it faded with each passing day.

With everything I felt, I turned it into food. Bellamy's absence left such a gaping hole in my chest that nothing else mattered. I was no longer scared to pull down my mother's recipes, and so I did. The loneliness from her death was still there, but it was like a scabbed scrape compared to the fresh wound of Bellamy's departure. Pretty hard to ignore how it felt like I was bleeding to death, my heart left exposed and torn to shreds.

"A little more coconut sugar, maybe…" I muttered under my breath, sprinkling the rich sugar over the top. Sweet, just like the hollow of Bellamy's throat.

"Sir?" Keith stuck his head into the kitchen. "Maria Tristov would like to speak with you," he hissed, his eyes wide.

"Why didn't you tell me she was here?" I snapped, anxiety twisting my stomach into knots. Damn. I thought she'd sworn she would never return. The entire kitchen froze, a held breath of expectation. This was the moment we had all been waiting for. Another chance to make a lasting impression, to save our reputation.

I took off my apron and slung it over the hook. Gave my hands a wipe. "How do I look?" I asked Joseph, and he leaned in and straightened my collar.

"You look good, boss." He wasn't looking down at his feet anymore, like he used to. He met my gaze, and I loved how clear and steady his eyes were. How certain he was. "You've got this."

"*We've* got this," I clarified. This restaurant wasn't just me.

Each and every staff member here helped to make it what it was. They each deserved a piece of our success, because I couldn't have done it without them. Without Bellamy...

I slowly made my way out of the kitchen and into the cool air of the dining room. Maria Tristov was seated at that same table... *our* table... where I had thrown Bellamy down and fucked him. He had promised me that there would be time for foreplay, but there never was. Our time had run out...

I tried not to remember how the air had chilled our skin, how he had felt beneath me, how his hands had clawed at me, urging me on.

I cleared my tight throat, swallowing the ache. "Ms. Tristov, a pleasure as always."

She gave me a sharp smile. "I would hardly call my previous visit a pleasure, but it's kind of you to say."

I lowered my chin in acknowledgment. "Fair enough. I certainly hope this visit has been more to your liking."

"Surprisingly enough, it has," she said, her smile widening as she gave her hands a little clap. "I must say, Mr. Badeaux, I returned to La Belle Compagne against my better judgment. I had written your restaurant off completely. But do you know... I kept hearing these little whispers over the past month, chattering about the changes you had been making, the new menu, the more vibrant décor. And I found myself doing something I very rarely did..." She rested her elbows on the table and steepled her fingers. "I changed my mind."

I could feel an unseen weight lifting from my shoulders. As many times as I had told myself that her opinion didn't matter, that she was just some critic who was paid to belittle and insult... I had been lying to myself. I did value her opinion, and I did care what she thought.

"The curry," she said, "it was phenomenal. Not quite traditional, but the perfect combination of sweet and spicy." She went on, raving about the various dishes she had tried, and a fresh sense of pride filled my chest. She wasn't just complimenting the dishes Bellamy had added to our menu, but some of mine as well. The ones that I had created since Bellamy left, the dishes I had infused with thoughts of love and passion in my heart.

"I am so glad that you gave us a second chance," I said genuinely.

"Quite." She offered her hand for me to shake, and I did so promptly. "Now how about some dessert."

"Right away." I returned to the kitchen feeling a million pounds lighter. "Joseph, please bring Ms. Tristov some dessert. Perhaps the strawberry square?"

"Of course, sir."

I caught a few thumbs-up from the staff, a pat on the back, but I didn't slow my steps as I walked right through the kitchen and into my office. This had been my goal, my destination, when I first approached Bellamy and his father. I had been trying to give my restaurant a fresh start. Mission accomplished. Except…

Did any of it matter anymore?

I sagged down into my chair and slumped forward onto the desk. I listened to the muffled sounds of the kitchen, and beyond that, the dining room. Everyone was enjoying themselves, laughter and banging pots joining together to create a kind of symphony. It was music… it was magic…

And none of it mattered.

I pulled my phone out of my pocket, hoping against hope that there would be a message from Bellamy. The screen was frustratingly blank. I could call Bellamy to tell him. Or I could text him maybe, just to pass on the good news.

My finger hovered over his name. Bellamy was free from me at last… I let him go, let him return to his old life, his family, his friends, his diner… and possibly his alpha…

If he'd wanted to talk to me, he would've contacted me, but he hadn't. Clearly that meant that he was doing fine without me. He didn't miss me, he didn't need me. I was just the guy who had bailed him out of a jam. If I was lucky, he maybe felt a little bit of gratitude for my help.

I should be glad to have helped. Bellamy and his father deserved every success.

And me? What did I deserve?

I would get a good review in *Yum!* magazine. That was enough… wasn't it? Love and a happily ever after? That just wasn't in the cards. Not for a man like me.

CHAPTER 19

BELLAMY

"Bellamy?"

"Pop!" I shot out of bed, but the room spun around and I grabbed the edge of my desk for support. Once the world stopped spinning, I staggered out the door and into my father's bedroom. The bed was empty. "Pop?" Did I dream he'd called me? And where the hell was he? He'd been stuck under the covers for nearly a month, the pneumonia having really done a number on his lungs.

"In here." The kitchen. He was boiling the kettle and bread was in the toaster. He'd pulled a stool up to the counter and was perched on the edge, dangling a tea bag in his hand.

"You shouldn't be up. Why didn't you call me?"

He grinned and patted my hand. "I did, but when you didn't stir, I got up. I'm feeling a little better. Not run-a-marathon better but more human, rather than a coughing, hacking, wheezing blob." Pop was a jogger, so when he made a reference to running, he was talking literally.

He pushed the hair off my face and tilted my chin to the left and right. "But you're the one who seems poorly. You've got no color on your cheeks."

The toast popped up, and I kissed his brow and got

peanut butter and jelly out of the fridge. His favorite. But on seeing leftover chicken soup that I'd made two days earlier, a wave of nausea wafted over me and I slumped against the fridge door.

"Bellamy?" Pop slid off the stool and shuffled over to me, his slippers sliding over the smooth wooden floor.

"I'm fine, Pop. Just need to catch up on sleep." That was a lie, but I refused to upset or worry him. He needed all his strength to fight off the damned pneumonia.

"Sorry, love. But looks like you've caught my nasty illness."

Maybe. Putting on a brave face, I ordered him back to bed. "I'll bring your breakfast. And then I'll go back to sleep. Send me a text if you need anything. Don't get up unless it's to go to the bathroom."

"Yes, sir." He saluted and shambled to his room.

Once he was out of sight, I sagged against the countertop and avoided the jars I'd taken from the fridge. My stomach roiled and I held the peanut butter at arm's length as I spread it on the toast. Same for the jam.

I managed to bring Pop his tray. He eyed me suspiciously, one brow raised as he put a hand to my forehead. "Go and rest."

"You sure?" It was difficult pretending to be okay when I wanted to curl into a ball under the covers and sleep the day away.

"Shoo." He picked up the TV remote. "My program's starting."

"Love you."

"And you," he answered as I left the room and collapsed face down on my bed. I pulled the pillow over my head, but then flipped onto my back, as being on my stomach was uncomfortable. As I lay still, hoping sleep would claim me but certain I might have to race to the bathroom and hurl.

At first, I assumed I had what Pop had and my lungs were

riddled with fluid or gunk. But I wasn't coughing or wheezing like him. There was no extra effort to get oxygen into my lungs or catch my breath. Instead, my gut was unsettled and sending me a message. I counted backward. When was my last heat?

I usually took time off during my heat, it wasn't safe for me to be around alphas who wouldn't be able to resist that primitive call to mate. Stuffing a sheet in my mouth, I counted on my fingers. Jesus, I hadn't had one while at La Belle Compagne. I would have remembered bolting the door at Larkin's house to keep me safe.

Shit! No one in their right mind wanted to be sick. Poor Pop had been on the verge of being whisked off to the hospital more than once. His gasping for breath, the lying on his belly at night, the agony of trying to get air into his lungs and the fierce grip of his hand on mine was something I wouldn't wish on my worst enemy.

But I was desperate for what was ailing me to be an infection. Not a bad one. Not life-threatening. Just a touch. How crazy was that? Because the alternative was… was… worse. Not for me. I would welcome the change, embrace it, love it. And Pop would be beyond excited. Ecstatic.

Larkin! This involved him. We'd had unprotected sex on a restaurant table. There were no condoms on the table beside the napkins and a vase of roses. Perhaps I should send in an anonymous suggestion on a restaurant review site?

Pharmacy! I had to get to a nearby one and buy a test. Could I pretend I was going to get more meds for Pop? Nah, I went yesterday. Fruit and cupcakes. We were getting low and I'd been tempting him with easy-to-eat yummy foods.

"Pop, I'm headed out to pick up a few things." He'd fallen asleep with the TV blaring and the remote clutched in his hand. *Perfect.* I scribbled a note and dashed out. Well, more like trudged, blinking against the bright light and scrunching up my nose as the odor of cooking bacon wafted from someone's window. *Get me out of here.*

On returning home, I crept into the house, hugging a paper bag, and raced to the bathroom. Five minutes later, I was sitting on the tiles, staring at a pink line that had upended my future. Not sure how long I sat there until Pop banged on the door.

With the evidence stuffed in my hoodie pocket, I assured Pop I was okay and headed to my room, needing to be alone. My nails were chewed to the quick as my thoughts went around and around, reminding me of water circling a drain. I had to tell Larkin. How could I not? Keeping it a secret would be a shitty thing to do.

When I first met him, he'd raged at the world. But in the time I'd been in his life, the fury inside him had mellowed, especially after we'd had sex and become closer. Did he want kids?

Thinking of Larkin brought up another problem. We hadn't been in contact since I left. He could have messaged me. *Ass!* I was the one looking after a sick parent. He was just swanning around the restaurant.

When I'd finally emerged from the fog of sleeping in a chair beside Pop's bed, taking his temperature and feeding him pills, I'd checked my phone. Nothing. Images of Larkin had drifted in and out of my thoughts during those long terrifying days when Pop was so ill, and I'd longed to hear Larkin's voice. Now it was too late. The distance between us was much further than the miles from his house to mine.

After it grew dark and Pop was tucked into bed for the night, I chewed over the possibility that Larkin would embrace me and this pregnancy. And what? We'd live happily ever after? Nah, not likely. He'd support the baby but want nothing to do with me? Or option three, he'd slam the phone down and I'd never hear from him again.

He should hear from me in person, but I didn't want to

leave Pop for long. My fingers were trembling as I punched in the word *Hi* and pressed send. Now came the waiting. And waiting. More waiting. Where the fuck was he?

Of course the phone beeped while I was heaving my guts out. Okay. Wash face. Rinse mouth. Pinch cheeks to give me some color. I read his text: *Hi. How's your dad?*

Not having the energy to write, I video called him. He might not pick up. Or he could be with another omega. His face popped up on the screen. He was scowling. We hadn't said a word and things were already going sideways. "Hi," I said.

"Hi." We managed one word each other, which was better than I'd expected on looking at his stormy face. "You look tired. And have you lost weight?" he snapped. Maybe that was the reason for the scowl.

I shrugged. "Looking after my dad. Haven't had time to eat or sleep much." I paused, hoping he'd ask about Pop again, and when he didn't, I added,"He's much better, by the way." Did that last sentence come out snarky? It did, I was sure of it.

Silence.

I miss you and I have something to tell you. So easy to say in my head. Impossible to voice my thoughts. I couldn't do it.

"The staff say hi."

"That's nice. I miss them." *I miss you too, but I can't tell you that.*

More silence, this one more painful than the last. And I was fiddling with a cushion on my lap, keeping my eyes downward so I didn't have to look at him. That face. Those eyes. Were they crowded with pain? Despair? Ambivalence?

"It's late."

"It is."

You're going to be a father. I'm carrying your child. But Larkin couldn't hear my inner voice. How could I tell him he was going to be a dad? Pin a note to his front door and run away? "I'd better get some rest."

"Me too." Our stilted conversation was finally coming to a bitter end.

"Bye."

"Bye." His one-word reply was barely above a whisper. The screen went dark. And I shoved that cushion over my face and muffled my howls.

CHAPTER 20

LARKIN

"That's it. Get out of bed. Right this instant." Randa stood over me, glaring down with her mom face in full force.

"Why should I?" I mumbled and rolled away—only to get blasted straight in the face with ice-cold water. "What the fuck!?" I sat up spluttering.

Randa gave a satisfied smile, empty glass still in her hand. "Since you haven't showered all week, I figured it would at least water down the stink coming off you. And maybe it might help snap you out of your funk."

A funk. Was that what this was? No, this was so much more than a passing phase of the blues. This was a piece of myself missing, cut out and stolen, never to return again.

I blinked up at Randa, and much to her disgust, I flopped straight back down onto the soggy blankets. "There's no point," I burbled, my face pressed against the dripping pillow. "Bellamy is gone and he's never coming back. The restaurant is in capable hands, and you have the house in order. I can just lie here in bed, and the world can keep rotating on without me. Nobody will even notice I'm gone."

"Grrr!" Did Randa just growl at me? I felt a hand clamp

over my ankle and then I was physically dragged out of the bed. I flailed around for something to hold onto, but other than wet fabric, I came up empty-handed. I landed on the floor with a hard thwack, my head bouncing off the wood.

"Get your ass up!"

I had never seen Randa so angry. In fact, since I was the one who signed her paycheck, she usually just left me to my own devices. What had gotten into her?

"NOW!" she roared, and I found myself bounding to my feet and standing at attention. "That's better," she said more softly now, brushing her hair back into her bun and straightening out her dress. As her face returned to its normal shade, it was almost hard to believe she'd let herself unravel for even a second, but honestly, the image of her blazing eyes would be forever burned into my brain, fuel for my nightmares.

She took a step closer and lowered her voice, but it still held an edge to it. "You will take a shower. Then you will get dressed. You will eat, and you will get some exercise and fresh air. Do I make myself clear?"

Alpha though I was, I found myself lowering my chin and muttering, "Yes, ma'am."

She gave a nod and headed for the door, and though I was tempted to just crawl back into bed, the fear of her returning to find me there was enough to get me moving.

Shuffle, thump, flop, drag. That was the extent of what I was capable of while throwing myself into the shower. The hot water pounding on my back did help clear my head a little, as much as I hated to admit it. I caught sight of myself in the mirror as I stepped out. I was like a ghost—or even worse, a ghoul. My skin was pasty, and there were dark circles under my eyes. I looked a decade older, at least.

Whatever. What did it matter what I looked like, when the only person whose opinion mattered wasn't here?

What else was I supposed to do again? Right, clothes. I

drew open my closet and front and center were my whites. My eyes went straight to the stain on the chest, a finger stroke of gravy. We never did soak the jacket that night… and I never wanted that stain to fade. It mirrored the mark he'd left on my heart, and if it was the only part of him that was left behind, I would treasure it forever.

I pushed the whites far back into the closet and grabbed some fuzzy pajama pants and a t-shirt. They didn't match.

Doesn't matter. My new mantra.

Regardless of my lack of care, the clean clothes also helped lift my mood. Next was food. I plonked down the stairs and into the kitchen, where the smell of bacon and eggs made my stomach growl. When was the last time I'd eaten?

I sat down at the small table as Randa put a plate in front of me. And just in case I hadn't gotten the message that I needed to participate in the meal, she picked up my right hand and stuck a fork in it.

"Okay, okay, I get it." I stabbed a bite of eggs and shoved them in my mouth. My tastebuds slowly began to come alive, and soon I was shoveling the food in with vigor.

Randa slid into the seat across from me. She'd been the housekeeper here since I was a child, but this was the first time she'd ever sat down at the table with me. There had always been a professional distance between us. Now, though, as she reached across and took my hand in hers, she felt more like family than staff.

And I found that I liked this feeling very much.

"Larkin," she said softly. Not sir, not Mr. Badeaux, but Larkin. "You have always been the most organized man I ever knew—even more than your father, and that's saying something. But you should know… it's okay not to be in control. It's okay not to have your shit together."

I looked up at her surprised. I'd never heard her swear before. Strangely enough, it endeared her all the more to me.

"I'm falling apart, Randa. Without Bellamy, there's no point… to anything that I do. How is that possible? We barely got the chance to know each other; why can't I just go back to how things were before I met him?"

Her eyes softened as she took in my hunched shoulders, defeated, beaten down. "But… do you really want to go back to how things were before?"

And that was the crux of the matter. Before Bellamy, I had been only half a man. I was struggling with life, with myself. I just appeared more put-together on the outside, but inside, I was like a desert. And then Bellamy walked into my life and showed me everything I was missing out on.

Did I want to go back? "No," I admitted at last. "I don't."

Randa gave a nod. "Right then. You need to get up. Brush yourself off and show that omega that you're worth coming back to. Even if it feels like you're just putting one foot in front of the other, you do it often enough and you'll soon find yourself running. You get back in that restaurant and find a way to make yourself happy. Why on earth would Bellamy want a man who doesn't shower, or eat, or get out of bed?"

"But… what if Bellamy is better off without me?"

"Bullshit," she snapped, and I laughed. I liked this new Randa.

I stood up and came around to pull her in for a hug. She wasn't my mother, not really, but it warmed my heart to know that she cared enough about me to play the role. Even though I was a grown man and should have been more than capable of caring for myself. I guess sometimes we all needed a reminder of the basics.

"Off you go now," she said gently, patting my cheek.

And so off I went. I pulled my whites out of the closet and headed in to the restaurant. Even if Bellamy didn't want anything to do with me, I would make him proud. He would see the rave reviews and know that he had set us on this path, that it was all because of him that we were able to rise from the ashes.

"All right, boss?" Polly asked cautiously as I walked in the back door.

I gave a slow nod, allowing the sounds and smells to surround me and buoy my spirits. "Yeah, Polly, I'm great. Thank you."

I set straight to work, helping out however I could, and when there was a lull, I pulled out my mom's recipes and some new ingredients to see what kind of dish I could come up with.

For Bellamy… and for myself…

CHAPTER 21

BELLAMY

"*B*ellamy, I missed you." Todd gave me a hug and I returned it. His brother Archie did the same, and their dad, Joe, patted my arm and echoed his sons' greetings. I was wearing a baggy shirt when normally I'd have on a tee. The boys didn't mention the slight curve of my belly which was disguised among the folds of fabric. And why would they? Though being children, they could just as easily have blurted out that I was getting fat.

Both Joe and his husband, Adam, flashed looks in the direction of my midsection. My pregnancy was still at the is-he-or-isn't-he stage. My employees knew, of course, and so did Pop. It'd been all I could do to stop him from broadcasting the news to the diner's customers.

We had made a trip to tell one very special person. My dad. One Sunday morning we'd driven to the cemetery and wandered through the headstones until we came to the one on a slope that had a great view over the grassy plot which was his final resting place.

We kneeled and Pop brushed leaves off the base and threw away the withered flowers he'd left here before he got sick. I waited until he'd arranged daffodils in the vase, thankful I'd convinced him not to buy roses. I couldn't look at them, and even a hint of their sweet fragrance had my stomach churning. Not so much because of the morning sickness but because their perfume took me back to the night Larkin and I had sex in the restaurant.

"Hi, Dad. I wanted to let you know you and Pop are going to be grandparents." I cupped the slight swell of my belly and Pop clutched my other hand as I continued, "Don't know if it's boy or a girl yet, but as soon as I do, I'll let you know." My eyes swam with tears. "And don't worry, Pop and I will tell this little one all about you and share some of the magical times we spent together." Resting a hand on the headstone, I added, "The baby is going to know you. Love you."

Being back in the diner with its frantic activity had me realize this was where I belonged. After leaving La Belle Compagne, I'd fantasized about taking the diner more upmarket, trying to attract a broader clientele with a fancy new menu, but it hit me that would be counter-productive.

People flocking to the diner were looking for comfort. They were seeking a safe place that wouldn't change from one visit to the next. And while we rotated dishes and introduced new ones, the staples didn't change. They were the same year after year. Eating here was similar to putting on a beloved pair of old slippers.

I arched my back and groaned as Danny said, "Take a break, boss. You've been on your feet for hours." He handed me a slice of fresh apple pie. Just out of the oven and still warm.

I wandered out into the diner to check on Pop. It'd taken him a few weeks to regain his strength, and even now, he wasn't working the long hours he used to. After convincing him to head home for a rest before the evening rush, I slid into an empty booth near the back, content to let the pie and the cushioned seat ease my discomfort. Putting my feet up on the seat opposite, I sniffed under my arms and made a face. I was sweating more than usual but had a spare shirt in the back room.

The baby was big enough for me to feel tiny kicks, and what should have been a joyful moment shared with a partner was tinged with sadness. Not only because I would be a sole parent, but also because Larkin was missing out. *And whose fault is that?* My inner voice cocked a brow and crossed its arms. *Quiet, you!*

I'd chickened out that night when we'd talked. *I'll tell him tomorrow*, I promised myself every night before falling asleep. But when a new day dawned, my courage had fled and I filled my day by doing things. Stuff. Anything to avoid confronting the guilt and the loneliness.

The bell at the door tinkled and I glanced up as a man walked out. If I squinted, I could almost pretend he looked like Larkin from the back. If Larkin had untidy hair and wore jeans that were so loose they showed the top of his ass crack. *God, I was desperate, seeing the alpha everywhere.*

I longed for the Larkin that eavesdropped that first night. He could be doing anything, really. Barking, bellowing, and stomping around hurling insults. I wanted him close by and yet I did nothing to make it a reality.

Weariness was pulling my eyes closed and my head lolled forward. The bell tinkled again, causing me to jerk upward and my eyes snapped open. A tall alpha blocked my vision. *Larkin?* My heart flip-flopped, but when I got a whiff of his scent—bitter like coffee granules on my tongue—cold fingers of disappointment crushed my excitement.

"Bellamy." Winston shoved my legs aside, but I pulled them back as he sat opposite, not wanting any part of me in contact with him. "I heard you'd returned."

"Mmmm." I stuffed the last morsel of pie into my mouth to avoid responding further.

"That looks good." But his gaze was on me, not the pie. My stomach turned as it used to when I was suffering morning sickness. But this was revulsion, not my hormones running amok.

"Last piece." *Liar!* "But I'll have Danny make your usual order to-go."

He stretched out his legs and his foot brushed over my leg. *Gross!* "I thought I'd stay and *eat in*." The tip of his tongue poked out between his lips as his eyes roamed over my face and chest.

Time for my escape. "I'll leave you to it. Gotta get back to work." I heaved myself up, but Winston grabbed my hand.

"I've never seen you dressed like this." He fingered the hem of my oversized cotton shirt. "I like it."

"Take your hands off me!" My voice was louder than I intended, and Sven, who was nearby, jerked his head toward me, and the customer he was serving peered over the back of the booth. Winston tried pulling me closer. "Stop it," I hissed under my breath.

"Oh, come on. I'm only having a little fun. You need more of that in your life, Bellamy. You're all work and no play."

"I play plenty." I yanked the shirt from his grip, half expecting it to rip. Winston's fawning over me had been going on for too long and I had to end it. There was one sure way to get the message across because he'd ignored the words I'd chosen in the past.

Sitting back opposite him, I lowered my voice. "Can you keep a secret, Winston?" His eyes lit up and I could practically hear, "Ding! Ding! Ding! You're the winner," in his head.

"Absolutely." He glared at the guy in the next booth who was hanging on every word. "Go on. You can trust me 100%."

I fixed my eyes on his face, wanting to enjoy the moment his brain processed the news. "I'm pregnant." There was no change to his expression. Ummm, didn't work. *Maybe he's a robot.* I was tempted to wave my hands in front of his face to see if he blinked.

"You're what?"

"I'm having a baby." *Not yours, so you can stop harassing me.*

"Pregnant?" *There it is.* He slouched forward and his jaw tightened as though he'd received a punch in the gut. I guess he had. An emotional one. He fisted the napkin and I sent that piece of cloth my sincere condolences.

"Mmmm." I changed the subject. "I'll get your food."

But he grabbed my wrist. If I hadn't been pregnant, I would have hurled him from the booth and kicked his sorry ass out. Instead, I used my words. Again. "Let go of me or I'll call the cops."

He shrank back. "Who did this to you? One of your staff take advantage late at night when you were locking up?"

"Stop it." I cradled my bump. "This is a much-loved baby."

His eyes were glued to my belly. "There is no one else worthy of you, Bellamy. If this was a mistake, I can forgive you. It's a tiny blip in what will be a lifetime of us."

"Look, I'm done being polite. Nothing I say or do seems to get through to you. Larkin is the baby's father. And there was no mistake, no forcing me to do something I wasn't comfortable with. I... I love him." I'd have to double back to that later. "And we are looking forward to welcoming the baby." *One of us is. The other has no idea.* "Now, do you want your food or not?"

He got to his feet, loathing in his eyes. "He will pay for this."

"What are you talking about? There's never been an us, Winston." *And never will be.*

"I will make that alpha pay for what he's done. For what he's stolen from me."

CHAPTER 22

LARKIN

I was dreaming of Bellamy, as usual. Just like every night, I was chasing him through a crowded kitchen. Staff kept crisscrossing back and forth in my path, causing me to trip over them or my own feet, bumping and jostling between them, calling out to Bellamy's retreating figure.

"Bellamy! Wait! I'm here!" Just when I finally caught up to him, I grabbed a hold of his shoulder and turned him around to face me. "At last!" I gasped, triumph inflating my chest.

He opened his mouth to reply, but all that came out was a blaring dinging sound. I was so confused. I could feel my entire face scrunch up. "What?" I asked. So, he repeated himself.

Ding, ding, ding!

I opened my eyes to find myself in bed, staring up at my ceiling. The room was nearly pitch black, except for an electric blue glow coming from somewhere.

"I don't—"

The ringing of my phone began again, and I wiped sleep from my eyes to roll over, plucking my cell phone from where it was lighting up the bedside table. "Hello?" I asked, still half asleep.

"Larkin?"

"Joseph? What's going on?" I slowly sat up, a little warning bell pinging inside my brain. I looked at the time. 3:27am.

"It's…" he began, and I heard a tiny hitch in his breath. "It's the restaurant. It's on fire."

My heart thudded sluggishly in my chest, as if taking a pause to understand what he'd said, and then it took off at a gallop. My veins flooded with adrenaline, and I was up and out of bed, halfway down the stairs to the front door before I'd even managed to pull on my t-shirt.

The drive over was a blur. I was directing my actions from muscle memory alone, left, right, slow down, go fast fast *fast*. The flashing lights were my first indication that I was getting close. The air was tainted with smoke. I pulled up the car along the curb a couple blocks away. I couldn't get too close, the street blocked by barricades.

I was stopped by a firefighter, but I explained who I was and I was escorted to a makeshift rally point nearby. "Joseph!" I cried out and dashed over as soon as I saw him. I wrapped him up in my arms, and he clung to my shirt, his tears quickly soaking into the fabric.

"I'm so… so sorry," he sobbed.

"Hey, it's okay. You're not hurt?" He shook his head but refused to meet my eyes. "You weren't in there, were you? It's late."

"No, I'm the emergency contact, so they called me first. I called you as soon as I heard."

"Hey, as long as everyone is okay, it doesn't matter. You understand? It was after hours, there was no one here. You're all okay."

He gave a slow nod, and I urged his eyes up. "What

happened?" I didn't want to ask, when he was clearly struggling with the event, but this was everything I had left and I needed to know.

"I-I don't know. I must have forgotten to make sure the stove was off," he wailed. Joseph was the rock of my kitchen, nothing ever flustered him, to see him this way was unsettling. "It's all my fault!"

"Joseph, look at me. You have never left a stove on in your life. You double-check everything, every single night. You have a checklist, that you literally check off. This isn't your fault. It was probably just some freak accident."

A look of doubt crossed his face, and his tears subsided a little. "Yeah... I did check off the list."

"There you go. It's okay, accidents happen. It's not like someone did this on purpose." As I pulled Joseph in for another hug, I caught a look being passed between two firefighters' faces. "What?" I asked them. "What is it?"

The man closest pursed his lips and looked over at his co-worker. "Well... I can't say anything for certain... this is off the record, you understand."

"Of course!" I snapped, and then swallowed back the instinctive rage when I felt Joseph stiffen in my arms. "Sorry, I mean, yes, I won't quote you on anything."

He gave a slow nod and lowered his voice, leaning in. "There was a man... he was seen fleeing the scene right before the fire started."

"What?!" It was like flicking a switch on my rage. For Bellamy's sake, I had been doing my very best to keep it all in line. Every time I felt even a little irritated, I would strap it down, take deep breaths, picture his smiling face.

Now? No, there was no reining this in. This was pure liquid fire running through my veins. I gently set Joseph aside, sitting him down in a folding chair, but I could see there was a flicker of determination in his own eyes. He'd heard what the firefighter said. And as I stalked off towards my restaurant, I could feel Joseph follow at my back.

No one stopped me as I walked down the sidewalk towards the restaurant. The smoke hung thick in the air, the smell dank and wet as they worked to keep the fire contained. Nobody wanted the whole block to go up. From across the street, I watched, my heart heavy, as years of work was reduced to nothing more than ash. Sludgy water flowed past in the gutters, and it was all washed straight down the drain.

I reminded myself that it was just material goods. I was insured, I could build again. The people who mattered were all okay. But I couldn't help but think of the stove, watching Bellamy work his magic with a wok. The walk-in freezer where I had last kissed him. The table where I knotted him.

As the water washed the remnants of the restaurant down the drain, I tried my best to convince myself that this didn't mean that my love for Bellamy was gone... we still had a chance... even though weeks had passed... months... and still no word.

I looked up, my eyes stinging from the smoke and tears. "Is that—" I began. There, across the road amongst a crowd of onlookers...

My feet began to move, the firefighter's words ringing in my ears. *A man... seen fleeing the scene...* Was it this man? What were the chances that he just happened to be here?

"Winston," I growled.

His eyes were glimmering with satisfaction, a sneer pulling at his lips, but when he turned to look at me, a whole new emotion crowded everything else out. Fear.

And he had every reason to fear me.

In my mind, Winston was the source of all my problems. This was all *his* fault. He started that fire, I was sure of it. And now he was sticking around to gloat over his success. Was he also the reason I hadn't heard from Bellamy? Was this man Bellamy's alpha?

This was the kindling for my fire, what brought my flicker into a blazing inferno of pure, uncontrollable rage. This was the force behind my fist, as it flew through the air and landed square in the middle of Winston's face.

Bones crunched beneath my fist and he dropped like a 200-pound sack of bricks. I would've kept pummeling him if I could've; it didn't matter if he was unconscious, I would make damn sure he hurt when he woke up again. But arms wrapped around me, hands subdued me, holding me back.

I found myself on my knees in the middle of the street, sobbing, Joseph's arms now hugging me as I had done for him just minutes ago. Police officers had appeared out of nowhere and were trying to make sense of the situation.

"Arrest that man!" Joseph called out, pointing to the man in a pile on the pavement. "He started the fire!" The officers seemed a bit confused, but they still went over to investigate, helping a groggy Winston to his feet before they began to ask their questions. Winston's eyes darted in every direction, looking for a way out.

Oh gods, I hoped it was so simple as that to catch the culprit. "You don't think Bellamy knew... do you?" I gasped.

"No." There was no doubt in Joseph's voice as he said it. "He would never."

I knew it in my heart, I did, but... as everything I knew lay in tatters about my feet, I couldn't help but feel a little niggle of doubt.

"Oh, Larkin, your fist," Joseph said sadly.

I looked down to where he was prying open my still-clenched fist. Blood was dripping off my knuckles from where the skin had been split. Probably on Winston's teeth.

"Come on then," Joseph said, helping me to my feet. "Let's go get you stitched up then."

So, even though no one had been hurt in the fire, I still somehow found myself sitting in the back of an ambulance.

An eventful night all around. Hopefully it would all calm down now, so I could just head home and fall into bed. I didn't think I could handle anything else.

CHAPTER 23

BELLAMY

A good night's sleep was something I longed for but hadn't had in weeks. Months, probably. Larkin was everywhere. In music blasting throughout the car as I drove to work. In the aroma of garlic smashing as I stood at the diner's kitchen counter. In a glimpse of a man wearing a suit similar to his favorite dark gray wool one.

But most of all, carrying our baby inside me. Whether the little one was kicking, hiccuping, or asleep, I couldn't banish Larkin from my head. Not that I wanted to. If I did, that would sever the slender thread that stretched from me to him wherever he was.

But I knew where he was. On the other side of town. I'd read the latest restaurant reviews.

Even though Danny was doing the early morning market run, my body hadn't gotten the message, waking up at the crack of dawn out of habit. Sitting in the kitchen sipping tea as the first light peeked into the corner of the room had me wishing things were different. Sure, I had Pop who was snoring softly down the hall. And the little one nestled in my belly who was currently asleep.

But a partner, a significant other. Someone to share the

burdens and the good times. Someone who'd prop me up when I couldn't withstand what life was throwing at me and vice versa.

The phone beeped and I almost ignored it. The market traders sometimes forgot I was no longer buying ingredients for a high-end restaurant and they'd put something aside and text me. But after glancing at the display, I grabbed it. Polly! I scanned the preview which read *Hi, Bellamy. Sorry to disturb you. Hope you're doing okay. I thought you'd like to know...*

Know what? Know what? She'd probably gotten a new job or a raise. Or the restaurant had another excellent review. No! No! No! Not at this time of the morning. I stabbed in the code, cursing I hadn't updated the device to a more expensive one with facial recognition.

... the restaurant burned down last night. It was deliberate.

Despair curled up my throat, almost choking me. And as I shot off the chair, my elbow bumped the cup and it fell onto the tiles, tea splattering my pajama bottoms while pieces of jagged porcelain scattered across the floor.

"Bel? Is that you?"

"It's okay, Pop. I broke a cup. Go back to sleep. I have to go out for a while." Pulling off my paternity tee, I grabbed up the oversized shirt I'd worn yesterday, discarded on the floor, and headed out the door.

Deliberate. The word wove through my mind. Surely Larkin wouldn't have committed arson in order to collect money from insurance. Short-tempered, arrogant, emotionally damaged he may be, but he was an honest man.

My thoughts raced as I contemplated different scenarios. I went from "Polly would have said if anyone was hurt. Wouldn't she?" to "Why didn't she tell me?" to "Oh my God what if Larkin's injured? Or one of the staff?"

I slammed on the brakes as I caught a red light and the car behind beeped as it came close to hitting me. Getting into an accident wouldn't be helping anyone. And the stress and adrenaline pulsing through my veins wasn't good for the baby.

As I rounded the last corner before the restaurant, what lay before me was very different from the view that greeted me every day for almost a month. Fire engines, hoses, pools of water, crowds gawking behind yellow tape, and the allotment where La Belle Compagne had stood was now a gaping hole with smoking wooden beams and a collapsed roof. I could see through to the alley behind it.

A police van blocked my way, and beside it an ambulance. Ambulance! *Someone's hurt.* Without giving a thought to my bulging belly, I dashed out of the car, glancing left and right for a familiar face until a hand grabbed my shoulder.

"Bellamy!" Polly's red-rimmed eyes and her anguished expression spoke volumes.

"P… P… Polly," I stammered. I hugged her, but as I held her tight, my bump came between us.

"Why didn't you tell me?" she gasped, nodding at my belly. "I wasn't expecting good news today. Not after this." She waved her hand at the smoldering mess behind us.

Not now! "Was anyone injured?"

"No. Not really. A few nasty cuts."

A paramedic, tending someone sitting at the back of the ambulance, bent over, and I caught a glimpse of Larkin, his hand bandaged, his shirt, face, and arms smeared with blood. The time we'd spent apart hadn't diminished what I felt for him but I'd never been able to put into words. Not properly.

He lifted his head, and I received a blank stare. But his eyes flickered in recognition and they lit up. *Larkin!* But the light faded as his gaze dropped to my belly.

"Larkin! I was so worried."

I outstretched my arms but dropped them to my side as his ice-cold voice delivered a statement in a monotone and he avoided my gaze. "Nothing to concern yourself with."

"What? Please, Larkin. La Belle Compagne has been

destroyed. Your life's work. Stop pretending and please don't shut me out."

His cool exterior and the steely glint in his eye told me I wasn't getting through. Instead of discussing the tragedy, we had to talk about the baby. But this wasn't the time or place to give him the news.

"I suppose congratulations are in order."

"They are." I folded my arms over the bump.

"Now I understand why you didn't stay in touch," he mumbled. "Was it the alpha I met at the restaurant that day?"

"Winston?" I spat out. "Hardly."

"That's a relief. Being a single parent is hard, but especially when the alpha father is in jail."

"What?" Maybe he'd had a bump on the head. "Who's in jail?"

"No one. Yet." He checked his watch. "Soon would be my guess." He stood up. "Whoa." He wobbled, dizzy, and I took his arm and sat him down. He yanked his arm out of my grasp. "I'm fine."

"You're not. I'll drive you home."

"I can do it myself," he spat out, reminding me of countless toddlers at the diner trying to feed themselves.

"You're going to make me do this here, aren't you?"

"Do what?" he mumbled as he picked dried blood off his face.

"The baby."

"Seriously? What? You're going to shove your pregnancy in my face? In the time I knew you, Bellamy, you were never cruel. Even when I lost my temper. You alway treated me with respect."

"And?" I asked, my voice raised, anger prickling over my skin. "This is no different."

"I don't want to hear about your baby daddy." He brushed an arm over his eyes. "I love you, Bellamy. I should have said it earlier before you ran off and found yourself someone else." He winced and rubbed a hand over his injured knuckles. "It's too late now."

Did I hear right? "No, it's not. You're wrong. It's never too late," I babbled and dropped to my knees in front of him, my bump protruding under the shirt. But I'd forgotten the ground was concrete. "Owww. Owww!"

"What are you doing? You're pregnant" He hauled me to my feet. "Owww! Owww! My hand."

I giggled despite my scraped knee because he loved me. He loved me! "There was never anything between me and Winston except in his head. This baby isn't his."

"Yeah, you said that already."

"It's yours, you big dummy." I expected something but not total silence. He shut down. No movement, no blinking, and no words out of his mouth. "I know this is a shock coming on the heels of what happened to the restaurant, but…"

"My what?" he asked.

"Are you sure you didn't bump your head? Look at me. Follow my finger."

"There's nothing wrong with my head," he snapped.

"Awww, there's the Larkin I know and love."

"Say it again," he pleaded.

"Ummm… there's the Larkin I know and love?"

"Not that. The other thing."

"Ohhhh, that." He reached out his good hand and put it over mine. "This is our baby. And I love you too."

"I'm sorry," we both said in unison.

"You go first," I told him.

"No, you."

"I don't know how to begin," I admitted

"Tell me you love me again."

"Oh, you." I bumped shoulders with him and he moaned. "Sorry."

"I should have called you but I was scared."

"Me too. I didn't know where to start," I said.

"Start is a good word. How about we rewind the clock and start again?" he suggested.

"We can't," I protested, my voice firm. Wariness crept into his eyes. "We go forward, not back. The past is full of mistakes and wrong turns."

"We're always going to make mistakes," he added.

"True. But we can avoid the ones we've already made such as not talking to one another."

"Awww, you two," Polly gushed as she raced over and hugged us.

CHAPTER 24

LARKIN

*A*nd move forward we did!

From that moment on, we made a conscious effort to communicate. We talked about anything and everything. Bellamy filled me in on all the awkward pregnancy details, from morning sickness to mucus plugs, and I... well, no, there was no way I could top the baby news, so I just blathered on about my dreams for the future, my speculation about whether the baby was a boy or a girl, whether their eyes would be brown or blue.

The insurance paperwork for La Belle Compagne was slow going, but I had savings enough to last a lifetime. My other restaurants across the state were doing just fine, and I could've moved closer to them, but honestly, they were largely autonomous and would only resent the grumpy boss swooping in and trying to wrest control of them.

But that wasn't the real reason I wasn't leaving... it was all Bellamy. I never wanted to leave his side again, not for one second. So, I went to work in the diner with him. It did wonders for my spirit, to be surrounded by the boisterous staff, the fun-loving atmosphere, plus Bellamy and his father, who insisted I call him Pop.

More important than business matters, Bellamy and I made up for lost time. We worshiped each other's bodies as if the meaning of life could be mapped out on our skin. But wasn't that the truth? He had brought meaning to my life, made every day worth living. And I planned to spend every minute being grateful for him.

"If you put your hand there by accident, then I suggest you move it. Otherwise, I might think you've got sexy plans in your head," Bellamy mumbled from where his head was beneath a pillow.

The hand in question was splayed over his bare ass, and was now slowly inching forward. "The placement of my hand is very intentional, I promise you," I nestled under his pillow to purr into his ear.

Bellamy's belly had gotten so big over the past months that it made sex somewhat more difficult, but we were always willing to adapt and experiment until we found just the right position. And it just so happened that he was perfectly positioned right now…

"Don't move," I told him as I slid down beneath the blankets. He was on his side with one leg propped up, and it so perfectly parted his ass cheeks for me. I ran my nose down the length of his spine, eliciting a shiver from him.

"I couldn't move if I tried," he groaned, but his groan quickly turned to a moan as I finally reached my destination and ran a tongue over his puckered entrance. I could feel the ring of muscle loosening under my attention, then clenching with want as I traced up his taint and over his balls with the tip of my finger.

Even though I'd told him not to move, he couldn't help but begin to squirm. He lifted his knee so I could reach through and gain access to his cock. As I tongued his hole and stroked his length, Bellamy's hips began to tilt and gyrate.

"Larkin," he gasped. "I need you inside me… please!"

"It's too close to your due date," I warned, but the hum of my lips against his skin just seemed to make him even more frantic.

"Bullshit," he snapped, grinding back against me. "The doctor said sex was still fine."

"And I thought I was the grouchy one," I teased, but as I said it, I emerged from the blankets and obliged my omega, lining myself up with him. "Pregnancy hormones have made you practically beastly."

There was no anger in my voice. No, the prospect of being a father had wiped my foul attitude straight out. There was nothing left inside me except patience and generosity. And a good thing, too, since my omega was currently very demanding.

"Now, Larkin! Now!"

Slick and saliva soaked his ass and I slid straight in with ease. "Yesssss," he hissed. "Now, move!"

I found his snarky lovemaking adorable. I smiled against the skin of his neck as he barked orders at me. "Slow… not that slow! Faster!"

His back was beaded with sweat, and I pressed my chest flush against him and reached around, running a hand along his distended belly. "I love you, omega mine."

"I love you too, alpha mine." He clasped my hand in his as we took a pause to just appreciate where we were. Not just my cock nestled perfectly in his channel, the warm wet squeeze of his muscles—though that was pure perfection—but teetering on the edge of parenthood. Together.

Bellamy and I had started as complete opposites, oil and vinegar, and somehow, we had found a way to defy chemistry and bind ourselves together, until the end of time.

I began to move again, in and out, our bodies rocking in tandem. Bellamy took our clasped hands from his belly and moved them lower, until both our hands were wrapped around Bellamy's dick.

As we increased our pace, a tingling began to spread from low in my gut. I tightened my grip on Bellamy's cock, and he gave a guttural moan. "Harder," he panted.

Whatever my omega needed, I would provide. My thrusts became frenzied, slamming into his ass, the slap of slick flesh a rhythm to our grunts and groans. Bellamy was close, I could feel it in the tightening of his already-taut muscles. Back and forth between my cock and my hand, he couldn't hold himself back from the double-sided sensations.

"Larkin!" he cried out as his body gave a final shiver, his cum spurting and coating my hand and the body pillow still wedged beneath his belly.

The feel of his warm cum on my hand was enough to tip me over the edge. My own orgasm released from my cock, filling Bellamy's ass to the brim with first my cum, and then my knot, expanding deep within him.

We lay there panting for a minute, allowing our rapid heart rates to slow and our breathing to return to normal. Bellamy gave a shiver, and I reached down and pulled up the blankets that had been kicked off at some point. "Better?" I asked.

"Much." He nestled back against me as we waited for my knot to dissipate.

"I have tamed the wild beast," I teased, pinching his bum, and he gave a wiggle, tugging on my knot. I quickly grabbed his hip to still him, or he would soon find me all too ready to go again.

When I was finally able to extricate myself from his ass, I got up and got the shower started. "Ready?" I called out from the bathroom. "If you're nice, I'll even wash your hair for you."

When he didn't answer, I poked my head back into the bedroom. "You okay there?"

"Huh?" He looked over at me, and there was something in his eyes. "Yeah. Sure. Fine."

I narrowed my gaze at him, assessing. "Uh huh. You know I don't believe you for a second, right?"

He pursed his lips and then held out a hand to me. "Little help?"

"Always," I whispered. I took his hand and helped him up from the bed and then to the shower. He was quiet as I lathered his back, massaging his aching muscles. Washed his hair. By the time I'd shut off the water and was toweling him dry, I was starting to get really worried. He still hadn't said a word.

"Okay, that's it. Tell me what I've done wrong."

"What? Wrong? Absolutely nothing! You've been a picture-perfect alpha. It's just…" A look crossed his face, and it reminded me of the time he accidentally forgot to set the timer and burned the pie I'd made. It was guilt.

"What is it?" I asked, suddenly alarmed.

"You know how I wanted you to fuck me…?"

"You mean this morning? Like, the sex we just had half an hour ago? Hard to forget."

"Yeah, well, remember how you suggested it was too close to my due date and I said—"

"Bullshit?" Like a coin dropping, everything he was implying came rushing into focus. "No! Bellamy, are you in labor? Did I make you go into labor?" My breath came out in a quick, panicked pant.

Bel quickly grabbed my face between his palms and brought my focus straight on him. "You didn't do anything wrong. But…" he bit his lip, and reluctantly admitted, "yes, I'm in labor."

That lit a fire under my ass, for sure. I raced to grab the hospital bag. "What are you waiting for? Let's go!"

"Uh, Larkin?" I looked up at Bellamy and then noticed that he was still naked from the shower. And not only that, but so was I. "Public nudity is frowned upon."

"Right. Yes. Clothes. Clothes are good."

So, it turned out my mad dash to the hospital was entirely pointless. Bellamy wasn't in labor. Just Braxton Hicks contractions. But I refused to have sex with him again until after the baby was born.

Now there were two irritable horny beasts in the house.

CHAPTER 25

BELLAMY

"Congratulations!"
"When's your due date?"
"I'm so happy for you both."
"Bellamy, you're radiant."

We'd barely made it through the diner door when regular customers besieged us, offering us their best wishes.

Just getting dressed—Larkin had to put my shoes on for me—and heaving myself in and out of the car were an effort. He had to open both double doors at the diner entrance to get me through.

My pregnancy had proceeded smoothly once the morning sickness was in the rear-view mirror. I had tons of energy in my second trimester and well into my third. But the past ten days had me counting the minutes and seconds until the birth. The little one had no room to move and had done all the growing there was to be done. There was no need to measure my belly or check the app that contained the week-by-week development chart.

It was time. The baby was ready.

Larkin was not ready. He was looking forward to being a father, something he'd written off in his 20s, assuming it would be denied to him. But getting from the late stages of pregnancy to holding a baby in our arms required a birth. And while he'd read the books and blogs, watched the videos and attended pre-natal classes, he wasn't prepared for the emotional roller coaster of being a parent.

Larkin led me to the same booth I'd been in when I'd told Winston I was pregnant. Winston who'd burned down La Belle Compagne and was now in prison with a long stretch of years ahead of him. He'd destroyed a building and a business but ironically had brought us together.

"What do you want?" Larkin asked, bringing me back to the present and banishing thoughts of Winston.

I closed one eye. "Is that a trick question?"

He shrugged and grinned. "Thought you might've changed your mind."

"Nah."

"One serving of apple pie coming up." He'd called ahead to make sure Danny was making a fresh one. He was. And cherry pie. My second favorite. He tucked cushions behind me. Something else that came with us everywhere.

I yawned and apologized as more regular customers greeted me. The familiar aromas in the diner, ones that formed a backdrop to my life, wafted around. Comforting but also bittersweet. Our extended family was looking forward to welcoming a new member, but there'd always be an empty space at the table. *Love you and miss you, Dad.*

"One slice of freshly baked pie for the gentleman." Larkin had added a scoop of ice cream.

"Mmmm. Decadent."

His brow furrowed. "Is that a good mmmm or a bad mmmm?"

"Good," I reassured him. He was attuned to the slightest groan or grimace and tensed when he thought I was in labor. "You're going to be great, you know?"

"At being a dad? I hope so. I didn't have a positive

example growing up." He stuffed a mouthful of pie in his mouth. "Or were you talking about the birth?"

"Both." I chewed my pie, letting the sweetness of the fruit mingle with the spicy cinnamon before continuing. "And yet look at you. You overcame all that negative shit."

He held up his hand. "Overcoming, babe. It's a process."

True. But the pie, one of my fav pick-me-ups—the other being sex and cuddling, both with Larkin—wasn't having the desired effect. I wriggled my ass, unable to get comfortable, and as Larkin tucked into his pie, the fork fell from my grasp and clattered onto the plate.

He froze. "What is it? More Braxton Hicks?"

My gaze dipped to the puddle of liquid on the floor and the soggy mess that was my pants. *Oh shit. This is it.* The baby had signaled it wanted out. "My water just broke."

"What?" He leaped up and banged his hip on the table. "Fuck!" Heads swiveled in our direction. "Pregnant omega coming through."

Pop, who had just arrived for his shift, took one look at the floor and yelled, "The baby's coming. I'm going to be a grandfather!"

The diner was a din of squealing and excited shouts while applause broke out as the staff and customers enthusiastically greeted the news.

"Your bag. It's at home," Larkin fretted. "Oh my gods, we left the bag in the house."

"I'll go," Pop offered. "And I'll meet you there."

"Thanks, Pop. No hurry, though. Drive carefully." I whispered to Larkin as he helped me up, "See? That was easy." Sven got the car unlocked and everyone waved and some blew kisses. But as Larkin buckled me in, a cramp wrapped itself around my belly. "Owww. Owww. Owww."

"What do I do?" he asked as his eyes darted between me and the car keys clasped in his hand. "Rub your back or drive?"

"Get us to the hospital," I panted. I needn't have worried about him breaking the speed limit and us having an accident. We crawled along the road and cars honked before finally overtaking us, and drivers shook their fists and yelled as they passed.

"Babe," I grunted after suffering through another contraction, "I love that you're driving safely, but could you go a little faster?"

He had white-knuckled the steering wheel and his unblinking eyes stared straight ahead. "I'm doing the best I can, love."

Of course he is. "I love you."

The contractions were closer together than all the literature had led us to believe, and I was bent over in pain when we arrived at the hospital. Once out of the car, Larkin transformed into the Energizer bunny. He yelled for a wheelchair and everything became a blur as I was raced inside, groaning, with Larkin holding my hand and issuing instructions.

Faces, shapes, noises, and that distinctive hospital smell swallowed me up as I was placed in a room and a doctor examined me. Not my doctor. She was on her way. I wanted to throw a tantrum. I didn't want a stranger to deliver our baby.

"You're five centimeters, Mr. Morley. So, a ways to go." Halfway and yet it felt like I'd run a marathon.

Pop had arrived and delivered my bag, which seemed to lower Larkin's anxiety level, though he fumbled with my phone as he attempted to find the playlist we'd made. "Better?" he asked as he put the air pods in my ears. "Can you see this okay?" The photo I'd chosen to look at wasn't a tropical beach or a tranquil lake. It was me, Larkin, and the staff at La Belle Compagne. It brought back such happy memories.

"Babe? Can you not check your phone? Whatever it is, it can wait."

"Of course." He tossed it onto a chair. "I was going

through my birthing checklist to make sure I hadn't forgotten anything. It says ice chips. I should get some."

That was sweet, but the contractions that were coming hard and fast didn't care about any list. They were the boss and I did their bidding. "Forget that. Just be with me."

The midwives suggested a walk might speed things up, so we traipsed along the corridor, stopping at intervals for me to rest my head against Larkin's chest. By the time I was ten centimeters dilated, I was flagging, my energy drained by the wrenching contractions.

"Time to push, Bellamy," Dr. Anderon, my doctor who had just arrived, told me after her examination.

"Larkin," I grabbed his shirt and pulled him closer. "You have to help me do this." All that existed was pain. My belly, back, legs, everywhere.

"Look at me," he insisted. "Bellamy." I had used so much energy to get this far, and my eyelids were so heavy, they were forcing my eyes closed. "You told me in the diner, 'You can do this.'"

"But," I gulped, and tears slid over my cheeks.

"No buts. You can 'but' later. Right now our baby needs you."

Dr. Anderson interrupted, "On the next contraction, push."

With my hand clenched in Larkin's huge fist, I bore down, expecting my body to be ripped in two. The contraction eased, and I flopped back on the pillow.

"Ready?" the doctor said. "Now, push."

There were brief respites amongst the pushes. It could have taken five seconds or five hours. Time had lost all meaning. Until... until there was a baby's cry. *Is that...?*

Larkin nodded, as he fought back tears. His trembling hands gripping mine as he gazed at the tiny squirming bundle in the doctor's arms. "Our baby."

"It's a boy. A healthy baby boy," the doctor announced.

He was placed on my belly, wet and red and covered in waxy stuff. Skin to skin. We'd become acquainted nine months ago, and now we were meeting for the first time. "Hi. You know me. You've listened to my voice and you're familiar with my scent. And you know this guy too. You'll remember his loud voice."

Larkin gave me a big grin as I wrapped my arms around our son and he rested his head on my shoulder and put one hand on the baby.

There was no need for words. We lay like that not moving, breathing in the same air as our newborn, who we were naming after my dad, Jeremy. We were officially a family.

EPILOGUE

LARKIN

"Order up!" I called through the window.

Sven came and grabbed the plate and offered me a quick wink. "Looks good, boss. Keep up the good work."

Boss. He'd called me boss. My heart gave a little contraction. After the restaurant burned down, I'd given up on being called boss again. I mean, sure, I could rebuild the restaurant with the insurance money, but it felt like starting over… and Bellamy had said we were only looking forward from now on. Besides, Joseph, Polly, and the other staff, they'd all found new jobs by now. I gave them all the most glowing references I could, and I was proud of their achievements. But… to be honest, I didn't think starting a new restaurant was something I wanted.

After Jeremy was born, it became abundantly clear that Bellamy needed all the help I could give him. Our son wasn't the best sleeper, so if I could help juggle all the naps and feedings, then nothing would bring me more joy. Saul, too, needed help. He wasn't exactly a spring chicken, and I'd noticed that his arthritis was flaring up, making it nearly impossible for him to balance heavy plates for hours on end. With me stepping in to fill in the gaps, he was able to settle into a semi-retirement. He would never back away completely, this was where he wanted to be, but now he mostly chatted up the regular customers. It was all a part of the diner experience.

Was this where I'd planned my life to end up? No.

It was better.

The diner would never make us a fortune, but we had no need for money. I didn't need to live in a mansion; I'd sold the house in favor for something more modest and family-friendly, just big enough for a few kids… and Randa, who insisted she come with me. She was a godsend to help with Jeremy while I was at the diner. I didn't need to jet set all over the world, either. Everything I could ever dream of was right here.

"Hey, babe," Bellamy said, stepping into the kitchen and dropping a peck on my lips.

"Hello to you too. And you," I said, turning my attention to Jeremy, who reached out to grab at my face.

"Busy day?" Bellamy asked. Even when he wasn't working in the kitchen, he couldn't help but pop in as often as he could. It was his nature, and this was his happy place.

"I think lunch is just gearing down. I'm sure we'll get slammed with dinner, though, it's that street market tonight."

"Ooh!" His eyes lit up, and I watched as he bounced back and forth on the balls of his feet, bobbing Jeremy in the sling strapped to his chest. "Maybe we could go?"

I gave a small smile. "Welllll," I drawled, "I dunno. I was planning on working 12 hours straight. Maybe I can stay open overnight too. Do you think there's a demand for overnight pie?"

He narrowed his eyes at me. "Okay, okay, no need to tease." He gave me a pinch on the ass on the way by, which was exactly the reaction I'd been hoping to get from him. He made the rounds of the kitchen, the staff all taking breaks to coo at the baby.

When he finally made his way back over to me, I leaned in for another kiss. "I was just thinking…"

"Yes?" He very much liked the ideas I came up with when I got to thinking. They usually involved the removal of clothes.

"Maybe after the market, Randa could watch Jeremy for a bit and you and I could have a pseudo date night."

He raised an eyebrow. "Pseudo?"

"Well, date nights usually involve going out… and I was thinking we could stay in." I waggled my eyebrows at him, just in case he was missing my innuendo.

He gave a sly smile and moved closer to me, sandwiching Jeremy between us. Our son gave a little giggle, and I dropped a kiss on the top of his head before giving Bellamy a more lingering kiss. "Make sure you take a nap with Jeremy this afternoon. You're going to need your energy."

I did my best to wrap my arms around my omega and placed my hands firmly over his ass.

"You're leaving floury handprints on my pants! Everyone will know what I've been up to in here." He gave me a half-hearted slap on the arm.

"I don't see anything wrong with everyone knowing you're taken."

"I'm pretty sure the baby strapped to my chest sends that message along quite well on its own." He gave me one last look over his shoulder on his way out the door, his eyes filled with light… and heat.

Tonight was promising to be absolute perfection.

∽

The day passed in a blur, as I found it so often did. The expression was exactly right, "Time flies when you're having fun," because I had to admit… this was fun! Somewhere along the way to becoming a business mogul, I'd forgotten the fundamentals, I'd lost sight of why I'd chosen to work in restaurants in the first place. Bellamy had brought it all back to the forefront of my mind.

Every day I spent in this kitchen, getting my hands dirty, brought the memories of my mother into stark clarity. My father may have been an absolute miser, but he had loved her too. After her death, this huge rift had opened up between me and my father, and in some misplaced attempt at bridging the gap, I had focused on the business aspect, trying to make him proud of me, instead of the love and comfort I'd once felt. I'd gotten lost along the way.

Bellamy was my map, my way home.

After my shift was over, I bade goodnight to everyone, waving at Saul on the way out the door. Bellamy would be here shortly so we could wander through the market stalls, but first, there was something I needed to do.

I pulled my phone from my pocket, and before I could second-guess my decision, I pressed a button and held the phone to my ear.

A click, then a pause on the other end. "...Hello?"

"Hey, Dad."

"Larkin?" His voice cracked. He sounded rough, older than I remembered him. "Is everything okay?"

Sure, I didn't call him on a regular basis... or ever... but he didn't trust that I was calling just to chat. "No, nothing's wrong. In fact, everything is finally right."

I spent ages on the phone with him, telling him about Bellamy, the restaurant burning down, and finally, about his grandson. He broke down in tears over this, shame and grief overwhelming him. He had let his own bitterness keep him from my life. "I promise, Bellamy, I'll do better."

"It's a start," I told him, repeating the words that Bellamy had offered me so long ago. "I can't wait to see where you go from here."

Bellamy gave my hand a squeeze as he appeared in front of me.

"Gotta go, Dad. I've got a date."

"Maybe I could give you a call tomorrow?" he asked hopefully.

"Absolutely."

Bellamy, Jeremy, and I walked through the stalls that lined the street. We sampled every food, we tried on silly hats and glasses, and as Jeremy's yawn got wider, we quickly made our way home for bedtime. Jeremy's that was, not ours.

No, we had hours left before we needed to sleep. "Come, love," I whispered as I took his hand and drew him down the hall and into the bedroom. "We've got somewhere else to be."

"You're lucky Randa is half deaf," he said with a giggle.

"Why? Are you planning on being loud?" *Oh yes, please, be loud*.

Instead of answering me, he closed the door behind him with a click. Then he slowly began to unbutton his shirt, stalking towards me.

My heart picked up its pace inside my chest. It wasn't just the fact that my insanely hot omega was baring himself for my pleasure—though that was most certainly a part of it—it was that I knew without a doubt, deep in my heart, that this was where I was meant to be. This was an accumulation of seconds, minutes, days, months… all for the promise of years. A whole lifetime of bliss.

This was our happily ever after.

BURNING BRIDGES

BY COLBIE DUNBAR & TRISHA LINDE

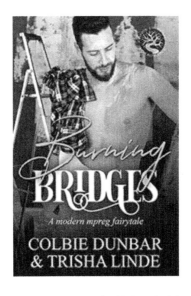

This gruff alpha has burned all his bridges... until he meets an omega who has him wanting to rebuild.

Alpha Cole wants nothing more than to be left alone in peace and quiet. Too bad there's a huge new condo development going up in his back yard. If it were just a bit of hammering, he could live with that, but it doesn't stop there. Oh no, it just keeps getting worse. Now they want his land, too. Well, you can forget it. His grandfather built this house with his own two hands, and there is no chance they're going to tramp all over his land. No way!

Omega William is the youngest and the smallest of his foster brothers, but that doesn't stop him from dreaming big. Together, he and his two siblings have started their own business, and they have just landed themselves a huge contract to build a new complex. It's a dream come true! If only it weren't for that house smack dab in the middle of the lot. No one seems to be able to convince the homeowner to sell, but maybe if William can get him to see some sense, maybe make him an offer he can't refuse…

Burning Bridges is the third standalone book in the Once Upon an M/M Romance series by Colbie Dunbar and Trisha Linde. With a mixture of knotty heat and scorching chemistry, Burning Bridges brings an overlooked fairytale to light, with a cast of lovable characters, such as foster brothers whose bond runs deeper than blood, an alpha whose loneliness has made him an outright troll, and an omega with a heart of gold who seems to be able to look beneath the surface. Billy Goats Gruff gets an mpreg twist, giving this classic tale a touch of heat, and obviously, a baby. Because what fairytale is complete without a happily ever after?

One-click now on Amazon!

NEWSLETTER SIGNUP

THANK YOU FOR READING. Please leave a review here if you liked this book. If you would like to subscribe to Colbie's newsletter, get updates on new releases and promotions, and receive a 6,000-word short story, *Ring In The New Year*, please visit her website here

https://www.colbiedunbar.com/my-newsletter-2/

To follow Trisha Linde, you can subscribe to her newsletter here

http://eepurl.com/ggRy11

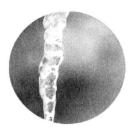

About Colbie Dunbar

My characters are sexy, hot, adorable—and often filthy—alphas and omegas. Feudal lords with dark secrets, lonely omegas running away from their past, and alphas who refuse to commit.

Lurking in the background are kings, mafia dons, undercover agents and highwaymen with a naughty gleam in their eye.

As for me? I dictate my steamy stories with a glass of champagne in one hand. Because why not?

If you would like information about newly-released books and promotions, please visit my website, Facebook page, Twitter or send an email.

https://www.colbiedunbar.com
colbie@colbiedunbar.com

ABOUT TRISHA LINDE

Trisha Linde spends all her time immersed in books, both reading and writing, mainly because she lives where it's too cold to do anything else, and what better way to keep warm than with a hot book. The first time she read mpreg, it was love at first sight, and there's no turning back now.

BELLAMY'S APPLE PIE

Dough:
- 2 ½ c flour
- 1c. unsalted butter
- pinch of salt
- ~6T water (just enough to make the dough workable)

Add flour and salt into a bowl and mix. Cut butter into the flour using a pastry cutter or food processor. Don't stress if you don't have those, two knives will do the trick just as well. Add water and mix until a ball forms. Wrap in saran and chill before rolling out, for at least an hour, but you can easily make the dough in advance and refrigerate overnight. Place the dough on a floured surface and roll out until 1/8" thick. Drape the rolled-out dough into your pie plate and cut away excess. Use the remaining dough to roll out a top crust, or cut into strips to use for a lattice top.

Filling:
- thinly sliced apples (I like to use a variety of apples)
- ¼ c flour
- 1T cinnamon
- ½ t nutmeg
- ¼ t cardamom

caramel squares (optional)

Toss the apples in the flour and spices to coat. Fill the pie plate to heaping. If you want to get fancy, you can cut up a couple caramel squares and put them in on top of the apples, before draping or weaving the top crust on top. Cut away any overhanging dough and pinch the crusts together around the edge. Don't forget to add a few vent holes to the top.

Bake at 375°F for 20 minutes, or until the top starts to lightly brown, then lower the temp to 350°F. Continue to bake 45-60 minutes, or until the insides are bubbling and gooey.

Note: If you have leftover dough, I like to make a batch of pinwheels. Flatten out the dough into a rectangular shape and sprinkle with cinnamon and sugar, but not right up to the edges. Roll it up lengthwise, keeping a tight curl, and then cut into 1" pieces. Place the pieces on a baking sheet and bake at 375F.

TOM KHA GAI

1" piece galangal or ginger, peeled

10 lime leaves or 1 T lime zest and ¼ cup lime juice

6 cups low-sodium chicken broth

1½ lb. skinless, boneless chicken thighs, cut into 1" pieces

8oz. shiitake, oyster, or maitake mushrooms, stemmed, caps cut into bite-size pieces

1 can coconut milk

2T fish sauce

1t sugar (palm, coconut, or brown)

2 stalks fresh lemongrass, tough outer layers removed (I totally cheat and use lemongrass paste that you can buy in the produce section)

Chili oil, cilantro, and lime wedges (for serving)

Using the back of a knife, lightly smash lemongrass and cut into 4" pieces. Smash or roughly chop ginger. Bring lemongrass, ginger, lime leaves, and broth to a boil in a large saucepan. Reduce heat and simmer for 8–10 minutes. Strain liquid into a clean saucepan and discard solids.

Add chicken and return to a boil. Reduce heat, add mushrooms, and simmer, skimming occasionally, until chicken is cooked through and mushrooms are soft, 20–25 minutes. Mix in coconut milk, fish sauce, and sugar.

Divide soup among bowls. Serve with chili oil, cilantro, and lime wedges.

RED CURRY

This recipe is incredibly flexible. I've made this with Indian curry paste and Thai paste, as well as trying out different brands of each. No two batches are the same, but they are always outstanding!

1T oil (coconut, peanut, or a light oil like olive or avocado)

½ lbs chicken thighs (or any kind of protein will work, shrimp or even tofu)

1 medium onion, diced

2t grated fresh ginger

1t minced garlic

Your choice of vegetables: broccoli, cauliflower, eggplant, snap peas, mushrooms. Whatever you have on hand, experiment!

2T red curry paste

1 can coconut milk

1T fish sauce or soy sauce

1T coconut sugar

1T lime juice

fresh basil leaves or cilantro, for garnish

This whole recipe takes no time at all to pull together

once it has started cooking, so I find it easiest to prep everything ahead of time. If you're planning on having it with rice, best to get that started too.

Heat the oil in a pot over medium-high heat. Brown the meat on all sides, and then set aside.

Heat the onions, garlic, and ginger until the onions begin to soften. Add a little water if you find that it's sticking.

Add vegetables and cook for a few minutes. Stir in the curry paste and cook for another 30 seconds.

Return chicken to the pot, along with the coconut milk, fish sauce, sugar, and lime juice. Mix well and bring to a boil. Reduce the heat and let it simmer until the chicken is cooked through and the vegetables are to your liking.

Serve and garnish with basil or cilantro.

BIBIMBAP

It takes quite a bit of effort to prepare and cook each element separately, but it's meant to be served at room temperature, so don't stress about keeping it warm.

<u>Meat</u>:

8oz beef (you can freeze a larger piece of meat just slightly, so it's easier to cut into thin pieces)

¼ of an apple, grated

3 cloves garlic

1T soy sauce

1T honey

2t sesame oil

Mix these together in a bowl and put in the fridge to marinate while you're preparing the vegetables.

<u>Vegetables</u>:

2 carrots, cut into thin wedges - fry for 5-8 mins

2 zucchini, cut into thin wedges - fry for 4 mins

1 bunch spinach - fry with a splash of sesame oil and ½ t minced garlic, squeeze to drain

8 mushrooms, sliced - fry for 2 mins with 1 ½ t soy sauce, ¼ t sugar, and ½ t minced garlic

4c. sprouts - fry with a splash of sesame oil, until just softened

Sauce:

Mix together in a bowl:

4T gochujang (if you can't find it, you can use a Thai chili paste in a pinch)

2T mirin

2T rice vinegar

1 ½ t soy sauce

2t sugar

1 clove garlic, minced

2 ½ t sesame oil

Fry the meat until cooked, and feel free to toss in all the marinating liquid.

To serve, fill the bottom of the bowl with rice, and then place a small amount of each element on top. Drizzle with sesame oil and place a fried egg on top and drizzle the sauce.

MANGO SALAD

2 teaspoons balsamic vinegar

2 teaspoons fresh lemon juice

1 teaspoon sugar

1/2 teaspoon salt

1/4 teaspoon black pepper

3 tablespoons extra-virgin olive oil

1 (1-lb) firm-ripe mango, peeled and cut into 1/2-inch cubes

1 large tomato, cut into 1/2-inch cubes

1 small red onion, halved lengthwise and thinly sliced crosswise

1/3 cup fresh cilantro leaves

Add balsamic vinegar, lemon juice, sugar, salt, and pepper to a bowl and whisk until sugar is dissolved.

Add oil, whisking until emulsified. Add remaining ingredients and toss until coated.

HERBED MUSHROOM PATE

"THE GRAY STUFF"

2T butter
1 lb. cremini and/or button mushrooms, sliced
2 cloves garlic, minced
1 onion, chopped
2T dry white wine
1 brick cream cheese, at room temp.
½ t salt
¼ t pepper
2t chopped fresh savory or thyme
1t rosemary
grilled soft flatbreads, crisp flatbreads, or crackers.

Melt butter in a skillet over medium-high. Add mushrooms, garlic, and onion, and sauté for about 8 mins. until liquid is evaporated and mushrooms are browned. Add wine and cook, stirring up brown bits, until evaporated. Remove from heat and allow it to cool slightly.

Place in a food processor with cream cheese, salt, and pepper, and puree until smooth. Taste to check seasoning and stir in savory and rosemary. Pack mixture into your choice of serving bowl. Cover with saran and refrigerate up to 5 days.

To serve, let pate stand at room temperature for about 15 min.

Makes about 2 cups.

Note: The flavors improve if made in advance and left for a day or two in the fridge. Goes well with grilled flatbreads or crackers, marinated artichokes, grilled sweet peppers, or pickles. It can also be used as a topping for baked potatoes, grilled steak or fish. Or mix with shredded mozzarella and use instead of tomato sauce on pizzas.

STRAWBERRY "SALAD"

SUBMITTED BY MIRANDA MARQUEZ

6 oz strawberry Jell-O
 2 cups boiling water
 2 1/2 cups salted pretzels (measured before crushing)
 1/4 cup granulated sugar
 8 Tbsp unsalted butter
 8 oz package cream cheese softened
 1/2 cup granulated sugar
 8 oz cool whip thawed in the fridge
 1 lb fresh strawberries hulled and sliced

Preheat oven to 350°F. Combine strawberry Jell-O with 2 cups boiling water and stir until completely dissolved. Set aside to cool to room temperature.

Crush 2 1/2 cups pretzels in a sturdy Ziploc bag, using a rolling pin.

In a medium saucepan, melt 8T butter then add 1/4 cup sugar and stir. Mix in crushed pretzels. Transfer to a 13x9 glass casserole dish, pressing the pretzel mix evenly over the bottom of the dish and bake for 10 min at 350°F, then cool to room temp.

When pretzels have cooled, use an electric hand mixer to beat 8 oz cream cheese and 1/2 cup sugar on med/high speed until fluffy and white. Fold in 8 oz Cool Whip until no streaks of cream cheese remain. Spread mixture over cooled pretzels, spreading to the edges of the dish to create a tight seal. Refrigerate 30 min.

Hull and slice strawberries then stir into your room temperature Jell-O. Pour and spread strawberry Jell-O mixture evenly over your cooled cream cheese layer and refrigerate until Jell-O is set (2-4 hours).

Printed in Great Britain
by Amazon